RETIRED

RETIRED

A Suspense Novel

BILL VANN

Heartlight Press
Albion, Michigan

Published by Heartlight Press
600 N. Clark Street
Albion, MI 49224

Publisher's Cataloguing-in-Publication Data
Vann, Bill
    Retired / Bill Vann. –Albion, MI : Heartlight Press, 2004

    p. ; cm.
    ISBN: 0-9729642-0-7 Hardcover
        0-9729642-1-5 (pbk.)

    1. Selling–Automobiles–United States–Corrupt practices–Fiction. 2. Drug traffic–United States–Fiction. 3. Insurance fraud–United States–Fiction. 4. Mystery fiction. 5. Suspense fiction. I. Title.

PS3622.A66 R48 2004   2003104027
813.6–dc22   0402

Book coordination by Jenkins Group, Inc. • www.bookpublishing.com
Cover design by Kelli Leader
Interior design by Linda Powers/Powers Design

Printed in the United States of America
08 07 06 05 04 • 5 4 3 2 1

To Janet E,
For all the years

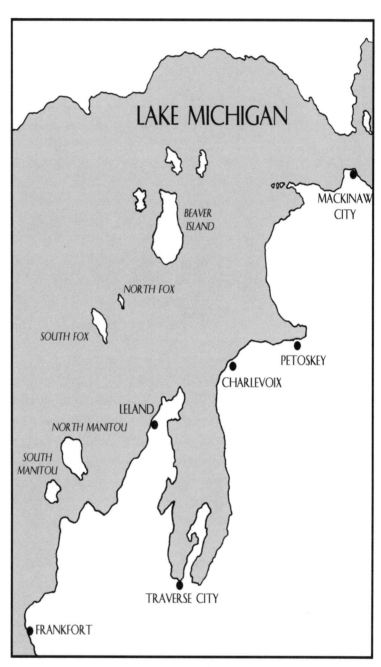

LAKE MICHIGAN

BEAVER ISLAND

NORTH FOX

SOUTH FOX

MACKINAW CITY

PETOSKEY

CHARLEVOIX

LELAND

NORTH MANITOU

SOUTH MANITOU

TRAVERSE CITY

FRANKFORT

NORTHERN LAKE MICHIGAN

PROLOGUE

It began with a newspaper article and a telephone conversation. She said, "I'll tell you how I found him. I read a piece about a Michigan car dealer who gave a speech. He proposed a consumer protection law prohibiting car dealers from using sales schemes: you know, first the salesman, then the manager, then the closer sort of thing. The pressure stuff. It was a one price fits all—easy on the buyer idea, and get this, he made the speech at a dealer think tank to a bunch of car dealers who were there solely to find new ways to screw the car buyer! Talk about balls, he was either bold as hell, or he was just awfully damned naive.

"I started thinking about this guy. I looked into him." She slowed her commentary. "He isn't a car dealer at all. This spokesman is a bookkeeper for a dealership. He has been there forever... thirty-five years. He has the background we need. He knows car dealerships and car dealers. He knows how they think and he knows how they act. And one more thing, he's retired. He has time."

"It sounds risky," was the response. "Not being one of us."

"What he must do is give us an expertise that we can follow," she replied. "That is what we don't have and what we must have. It is totally absurd, but the fact is that thirty million people go into car dealerships every year, and nobody knows a thing about them. Nothing. Zilch. No one.

I talk to the I.R.S., they audit, they chase the money, but they admit to knowing absolutely nothing about how these people operate. The F.B.I.? Not a thing. Nothing. No clue." She would have continued, but was interrupted.

"Let me ask you this. If it works, do we make this person a part of it?"

There was a moment of silence.

"Hell no, about making him a part of it. Hell, no! This is our baby. Our first big chance. We've got to make it work. Work for us. Remember that, you and me. No one else. Period!"

There was another pause and she returned, bluntly, "*If* it works we will use him. Use him," she reiterated, ending with an upbeat, "I'll plot this out."

"Good luck," was the answer. "I'm ready."

That was the telephone conversation. Later that evening, in her apartment, she sat at a desk, legal pad in front of her; loose cigarettes scattered about the desktop, and worked a plan. It lasted well into the night; it was as if she were an architect designing the unusual, taking something almost totally abstract, and making it real, and making it workable. And that was only one of her attributes.

PART **ONE**

She preferred to be known as Alice Henrietta. She was an intelligent, energetic lady, but she was not an intellectual. She thought of herself as being driven by ambition. Now, in her ninth year and third show of the season, Alice Henrietta was considered the most successful arts and crafts dealer in south central Michigan. Certainly the most energetic in Jackson County. This year's coup de maître was a small, four-by-five inch, stained glass hanging created in several colors and designs. Some were round; many were oval; some even rectangular. Some heart-shaped. All leaded.

The unlettered stained glass was produced by two male schoolteachers from Ann Arbor. They lived and worked together, loved their art, and felt they were indeed a small part of a creative genius. Someone for the ages.

Alice Henrietta painted the words *carpe diem* on them. She considered herself a calligraphist. As she would say, it was the artistic part of her work. The lettering was on one side of the glass, and her initials, ever so small, were on the other. Initialing was very important to her. It was her statement.

Before each arts and crafts show, hundreds of pieces hung from every beam of her beamed-ceiling workshop, which included the living, dining, bedroom, and kitchen area of the home that she shared with her husband of thirty-nine years, Harry Jones.

Toward the celebration of his wife's talent, Harry was given only one job. After the lettering dried on each piece, Harry wrapped the stained-glass hangings in soft paper and inserted them into a small but elegantly-printed bag. The bags were flowered, with handles on a background of Tiffany blue. Then, with marker pen, he would denote which shaped piece was within each bag. Alice checked his work. Harry never asked and was never told what *carpe diem* meant. Nor did he care.

Alice Henrietta didn't aggravate Harry as she might another husband. This was due more to Harry's nonchalance than any sort of pseudo-obedient behavior on her part. In a wearing sort of way, each of her self-acclaimed successes seemed to amuse him. It didn't surprise him when, a few years before his retirement, she bought a small house, then painted, decorated, and furnished it with her creations, then sold it merely because she always wanted to be an interior decorator. That she made a profit didn't surprise him either. It only left him slightly bewildered by all of her energy.

She bought two more houses that year, a sabbatical from her arts and crafts. She did most of the work, asking little of Harry. Deep down she knew he couldn't pound a nail in straight, and rather than teach him, she let it go. She made that fact known to more than a few of her friends, in a rather cavalier sort of confidence, that her yearly income had now surpassed poor Harry's. Her friends, not Harry's; he had no close friends. He only knew about the income business because, being an accountant, he did the family taxes.

Harry did aggravate Alice Henrietta. Years earlier she had talked incessantly about his lack of ambition. She had asked if being a bookkeeper/office manager at the car dealership had ever gotten to him? Hadn't he ever wanted to have a small dealership of his own? Any kind of business? Or, digging deeper into him, didn't it ever just irritate the devil out of him when others were promoted over him for the bigger jobs? The "paying jobs," as she put it. How many managers had come and gone during those thirty-some years?

Early on, Harry would just nod, rarely offering a defense, except to say that his job was unique—vital to the business. Later, when cornered, he would look calmly into her eyes, as she quarried, and repeat defensively, in a monotone, "Yes, Alice, how many have come and gone in those high paying jobs? How many were fired? How many forced retirements? How many lasted through four owners and six recessions?" Explaining to Alice Henrietta about retirement and the future, that he'd rather save than risk, helped little. Finally, after Harry had explained and defended for enough years, Alice grew tired of pushing. She'd rather just push herself.

Bookkeeping was a logical kind of business that fit Harry well. Things were either black or white. When matters became gray, as they often did in the car business, Harry's opinions were rarely sought. So the generalization surrounding him was that he was a non-opinionated egghead. It was actually one of those "was the tail wagging the dog, or the dog wagging the tail" questions. Other bookkeepers, even the factory people, often called him regarding the mechanics of the job, but nobody ever asked him for his opinions. He wasn't in that business.

Only once did he deviate from his confined domain as the bookkeeper. With the encouragement of an atypical dealer, a truculent individual who thrived on friction, Harry represented the dealership at a national dealer "think tank" seminar and proposed a frightening idea, his dealer's idea—the elimination of selling schemes used in auto dealerships. Outlaw the bartering and replace it with one price, non-confrontational merchandising, similar to the big discount stores. The upside would be a more comfortable buying atmosphere, greater customer satisfaction, and, ultimately, it would create a new change of attitude toward dealers. Downside, it would cost dealers millions in profits now generated by all the sales gimmicks.

The idea caught on. It bolted from the seminar to the National Dealer Association to the press. They named it "one price shopping." It got Harry quoted in *The Post*. He was championed by the car manufacturers; vilified by the twenty-three thousand U.S. auto dealers. For two weeks Harry was either complimented or scorned. He was badgered well beyond his limited capacity for criticism. He felt he'd been had; he lost control, and in a confrontation with his dealer, swore he'd never get caught up in a deal like that again. The exposure didn't do a thing for Harry. It was all the limelight Harry needed in his life. And it wasn't even his "damned" idea.

The strange thing about Harry Jones was that if he'd made a success of himself, no one would have been surprised. It was only the fact that he had been moderately successful, a failure to those who had cared, that baffled. Of course, that was in the past, when there were those who cared. As his father advised, "Harry, before you're forty, everyone wants to help you. Take the help, Harry. Because after forty, nobody's interested. Nobody has the time."

Perhaps Harry was one of the many who turned forty just a few years too early in life.

As the "thoroughbred" people would say, he had the lineage. Sired by winners, front-runners, and stretch-runners. The bloodline. His father had been an excessively dedicated workaholic. An overbearing man, both physically and mentally, he out-worked, out-maneuvered and out-brained his way to the C.E.O. position of a large company. He was a man with aspirations. Unfortunately, they were mostly for himself.

His father's unnerving presence caused business as well as social acquaintances to shy away from closeness, and it had the same affect on his only child. He did have one goal for his son. Lacking a formal education, he was determined that Harry have a college education and a degree to show for it. And none too soon for Harry. After high school graduation, he was off to college and gone forever, rarely returning home. Even to see his mother.

His mother had been an original—self-willed, a child of the twenties, a young adult of the Depression era. With a social worker's background, she had become a prominent politician when few ladies dared the challenge. As a patron of the poor, she was as highly regarded as anyone within her sphere. Unlike her husband, she had high hopes for Harry. A protective type, who, seeing him perform in drama, as a debater, and as a serious student, dreamed a career in the arts for him. But Harry disappointed his mother. After an early fling as an English major, he found he was much better with numbers than words and left higher education, a mediocre student, with a two-year associate degree in accounting. No one was happy with Harry. Not even Harry himself.

About that time, he met his future bride over roasted marshmallows while ice-skating at a lighted city park. They were married without fanfare. His father, having been asked about the bride and groom, referred to them as "a couple of nerds in a snow storm." His mother was not amused.

Harry was in his early forties when his mother and father died. He inherited a small estate. Nothing that he could retire on, but enough to offer a slight security. Enough to send two daughters through college, enough to give each a start. He was given some small credit for this gift that he accepted. Alice gave him that much, too.

Alice's aggravation about Harry's lack of success never turned into a taunting affair. It could have except for one decision by Harry that forever quieted his wife's anxieties, though perhaps much too late for Harry's sake.

It was one of those uncharacteristic decisions that few ever make, all wish they had, and most spend the rest their lives shaking their heads over. It is quite often a snap decision, because deep thought screws up a lot of good decisions. It always did for Harry. Contrary to the conservative nature of Harry Jones, it sprang from God knows where, unthinkable even after the fact. The kind of decision that changes lives. It changed Harry's life, his character, and it put a spark into his soul that would later ignite a willpower no one even knew existed! For sure Harry didn't know it existed. Later on he'd find it in the strangest ways, and in the oddest of circumstances. But all that was later.

It was at the Chrysler dealership. It was the end of the month, the financial statement completed. He was through shaking his head, as he often did at the money someone else was always making. Harry glanced at the stock page of the *Citizen Patriot* and noticed Chrysler stock at ten dollars a share. Bad news, talk of bankruptcy, had driven the stock down. But Harry had a feeling about the stock. He had seen Chrysler near disaster before and often regretted that he hadn't the nerve to invest years earlier when the stock took a meteoric rise from oblivion. That earlier lack of willpower probably irritated him more about himself than anything else. A failure of will, damn it, his father would have said. A failure of will! A failure of will, he repeated to himself, as he rose. Erect in both posture and composure, he pounded on his desk.

"The complete hell with it," he shouted aloud, for no one to hear.

And he made a decision.

"I'm doing it."

Harry took the next morning off, a half-day of his one day of personal time allotted each year. He withdrew his inheritance from its several accounts. He cashed his bonds, even mortgaged the home, and with most everything he and Alice Henrietta owned, on a quiet Saturday strolled into a discount brokerage house with one hundred and sixty thousand dollars, and put a buy order in for fifteen thousand shares of Chrysler common stock. Everything was surreal. On the trip home he stopped at a White Castle, ordered a bag of sliders, two large cokes to go, and very uncharacteristically burst into the house and called for Alice to come to the table and sit down. He offered her half of his bounty, which she refused. He told her eye to eye what he had done, asked if there were any questions and, not waiting for a reply, confidently rose, and with no apparent remorse, only a growing stomach ache, marched off to his room and went to sleep.

Secretly, Harry was not all that casual about his investment. On the corner of his desk pad at work he recorded in fine print every movement in the stock.

March 8, 1/4 at 11 1/4
April 10, 1/2 at 11 3/4
'91 went into '92.
February 16, 3/8 at 14 1/8

Alice often asked Harry how the stock was performing. Quite often, in fact, especially after she found that he had mortgaged her workshop! As the stock rose, however, he even volunteered the good news. He became more confident, almost flippant, as it quadrupled into the forty-dollar range. In early January of '94, Chrysler stock hit sixty-four dollars. Harry asked for another half day of personal time. Five days later he received a check for nine hundred and sixty thousand dollars.

Alice Henrietta and Harry didn't talk much about the money. She did ask once if he had a plan and before she could catch herself, he looked calmly into her eyes and said he knew one thing: he wasn't investing in a car dealership, period! There was something in his tone. Perhaps a challenge. Perhaps a settlement. And it hardly came up again.

I t is not an overstatement to say that for many retirement comes as that most monumental in the hierarchy of life's important events. Whether or not other goals are reached, this one is attained. Whatever commitments are kept, desires gratified, retirement is proclaimed an accomplishment; met outwardly with a feeling of pride, inwardly, more like a feeling of relief. The retirement planning period lasts more or less as long as the working phase, usually intensifying during the later years as other goals become less attainable. Say for the last twenty years.

For Harry there was nothing blessed about retirement. There was no celebration. When he retired it was of no consequence to either him or his employer. In fact, as he approached his sixtieth year, the hint was clear; he was expendable. He suspected it was inevitable. He blamed no one. And he felt no desire to stay. So one day he just went home. He had no need to continue working, or so he thought, certainly no financial need. He did get job offers and that gave Harry a good feeling. It reinforced what he already knew; that he'd been good at what he did.

Like everything else about his life, he had made no real plans for retirement, never thinking about the changes it would make in him. What retirement changed most about him was time; it worked against him. His job had had a control over Harry, as it does over most, and suddenly it was no longer there. Time and control and even blame were essential parts of his life, and now they ceased to exist. Time became irrelevant. There was just no need to account for it.

Harry, more than most, was motivated by habit. At 6:45 a.m. he was up and in the bathroom shaving. After shaving and before dressing, while Alice Henrietta was still asleep, he would set the automatic coffee maker, fill it with two table-spoons—one of crème de noise decaf, one of hazelnut regular. For years the mixture had suited him fine. It worked well with his exercise machine. Then a quick shower. After a breakfast of bran flakes and grapefruit juice, another cup of coffee and CNN news. He doubted the bran was actually good for him; it merely filled him so he wouldn't eat any-thing more fattening. Then he would put on his dark suit, say good-bye to Alice, and he was ready to start his day.

Only now he didn't put on his suit anymore. His day had ended at 7:25 a.m.

The first few months had an almost dehumanizing effect on Harry. There was no month-end report, no Monday con-ference with fellow managers, no confidential cost analysis for the general manager and the owner. Not even a quarterly corporate tax to pay. The sense of responsibility was gone. Nothing to consume him. The irritable thing now was not being able to find anything to get irritated about, only small inconsequential nothings, and the awful attempt to magnify something that wasn't anything. Non-events became events. When putting the garbage cans out for Tuesday morning pickup became Monday night's major event, Harry knew he was in big trouble. There was a huge void. It seemed to him that everything was up and running except him.

After his retirement, Alice Henrietta did so wish he would take up a hobby. He was around the house—the workshop—much too much. She had worried not so much about his retirement as just having Harry around all the time. "A hobby, Harry. Do something! Please just do something."

What it came down to was that Harry needed to find the answer to his problem. Now that he'd backed into this dismal, self-inflicted state of retirement, exactly what the hell was he going to do with himself for the rest of his life? No ring of self-pity to it. There was no self-pity in him. Harry had kept a diary. Reading it, one would have known there wasn't a hint of self-pity about him. He had kept a diary for almost as long as he had worked, although he didn't call it a diary.

It was his log. More like an extension of his bookkeeping, except that he didn't make daily entries; only important events, important thoughts. A monologue in print. Alice Henrietta knew of it, knew it was prestigious in size, but had no desire to explore. She hardly felt there would be anything titillating about it. He never talked to her about it, at least not since she described a diary as nothing more than a self-portrait by someone without a talent to paint or too cheap to buy a roll of film. The girls, having once peeked, told their mother it was, "Full of blah, talking about work and barometric pressure and stuff like that." The day he stopped working he entered this into his log: " Sunny, high cumulus, spectacular thunderheads, anvils and all, maybe another front approaching." His relationship with the weather station wasn't the answer to his problem.

Although Harry didn't need to refresh his thoughts concerning his present dilemma, he often browsed the log. A feather was placed in a recent entry.

Sun., May 16. Rain. Once again it has come to be a full house of busy women. Alice Henrietta's people everywhere, every weekday of every week. Now the arts and crafts season is in full bloom. I've found a room, however, where I can be alone. Only the upstairs bath gets a little cramped with Forbes, the Wall Street Journal, *and* Business Week. *The TV's a slight problem. But if I'm really lucky the weekend won't pass without the crying grandchildren, irritating the bejesus out of me. Oh, well, I long ago decided that I'm too old to be a father and too young to be a grandfather. Really it isn't the irritating wailing grandchildren who're the problem anyway. It's their goofy parents. Either too much*

*attention or not enough. And too many aspirations. Jesus Christ,
they're only three, five, and seven! All for the wrong reasons, anyway. Parents raising children—worlds' big problem. Sum and
substance. And son-in-law! The son-of-a-bitch. Fathers-in-law
know nothing about anything and never will period thank you,
you prick! My vocabulary is taking a turn, has an abrasiveness
about it since I retired. Is that what it has come down to?
Continue on Monday:*

*Mon., May 17. Still rain. Rain sleeve shows two in.! Consider
the second daughter the single one! Due to my newfound presence, I am now privy to problems I've never heard discussed, knew
existed, experienced; had not even read about while waiting with
Alice Henrietta at the supermarket checkout! Men friends,
women friends—no friends. Simple suggestion? "My dear, get a
cat, feed it, and—Christ Jesus— it will love you for life!" But as
a solution??? Of course this called for deeper analysis— dialogue
over dinner, discussions with the shrink, sessions at the therapy
group. All of which is to say, ultimately, my suggestion was
nixed! As is every suggestion about anything. I have now conceded that I am the focal point for bad suggestions. P.S.—jobs
around the house created specifically for me. Never, ever initiated
before I retired. How the hell did the place stay together before I
retired and haunt it for twenty-four hours a day? I am not an
electrician, plumber, heater-man, carpet-cleaner, or never want to
be! Capitalize that!*

Every hour of every day Harry thought about his problem. It was like a disease that was spreading fast. He was suf-
focating from retirement. What he began to realize was that
in his bookkeeping job, in his own office, at work, there had
been a privacy about it that he no longer enjoyed. He thought
about his situation and that of the hundreds of thousands of
mid-level people who don't realize that working in their
undersized, cluttered, stuffy working cubicles probably
grants them the only real privacy of their lives. It was hardly
conventional, sound thinking, but he found it was so.

About those job offers he'd received? No goddamned way. Harry would fight it. He was retired. And those ladies! Alice Henrietta's new partners in the house were energized, loving work. Christ, why didn't they retire and go home to their retired husbands. But then it would be back to Alice Henrietta's wish, "Please, Harry. Something?"

Remarkably, Harry did do something. Alice Henrietta's wish came true.

A lighthearted scheme. But a slight wink at the devil.

Strolling one day, thinking about everything and nothing, Harry noticed a "for rent" sign in the recessed corner doorway of an old office building. The front of the building had been restored by its current occupant, a title and mortgage company. Gold letters embossed on a facing above the arched-top French doors gave a certain prosperity to the business. Catching his attention above the rent sign was an eye etched in the frosted glass door, A large eye, almost as wide as the antique door itself. A look of opulence in an otherwise dingy door well. Possibly designed for an optometrist, the door and its eye beckoned Harry. The cornerstone was dated 1881, probably also dating the door and its casing. He hesitantly stepped through the unlocked door onto a banistered stairway. He opened the upstairs door into an empty office. The walls were oak, wainscoted, paneled to the ceiling. A high ceiling. The small room, Harry thought, appeared somewhere between an expensive yacht club anteroom and a lawyer's office without books.

He was entranced. A secluded place for himself. Away,

but not too far away. Alone at last! A secretive place of leisure. A place, he felt, that would halt his retirement blues. He would decorate it with a large desk and deep-seated chairs, subdued lighting, and several antiquarian prints. A coat rack. A small computer. A statement piece, though, would be necessary: An armoire, huge, taking up a quarter of the wall, reaching to the ceiling, filled with brass cups, leather books, a trophy, even a glass-framed picture or two of the grandchildren. Harry's imagination was ecstatic.

That evening talking to Alice, he was cautiously under-whelmed. He informed her of his intent for the office. A quiet study place for his "stock things."

They both agreed, but only if the rent was right. Harry made sure the rent was just a little less than Alice would have approved.

"That is *so* low, Harry," she exclaimed in front of her fellow crafters.

"Why, at this rate, I could afford a shop of my own," she beamed at her confederates. Harry frowned, keeping the truth to himself.

"How did you ever strike such a deal?" She returned to her stained glass. Artfully, he thought, as he left the room to the hive of crafters. She would write the monthly check and he'd pay the difference in cash.

Down came the rent sign and in its place a tastefully designed brass plate. It said *private*. He liked it. It wasn't a *carpe diem*, but he was sure Alice Henrietta would approve.

Harry was transformed. The depression over retirement was exorcised and time, the enemy, was now his friend. He was possessed by the spirit of entrepreneurship. Sitting before his computer or reading his *Forbes* or checking the daily charts and stock quotations, he had become a money manager... at least in thought!

As a financial advisor he spent hours devising portfolios for clients. Then he would counsel. Leaning well back in his deep-cushioned leather chair, cautiously eyeing the two empty leather wingbacks across from him, he painstakingly presented his plan. Sometimes tapping a pencil on the desk, a trait of his, other times standing over his clients, lecturing. Proposing a master plan. A plan to quadruple their holdings. He was an expert. They nodded approvingly. He was a master salesman; congenial, but firm. They were eager to pay for his services. His commission. Ending a meeting, he would walk his clients through the office, like a tour guide through a gallery, proudly pointing to pieces of the décor that particularly pleased him, knowing these clients would refer him to other potential clients.

How would he handle his growing clientele, he asked himself. In fact, he needed a newsletter. He would acquire a copyright. Quarterly, no, monthly, it would be sent to each client. Plus several hundred more newsletters to selected subscribers. A ghost letter for ghost clients, just to gain a small bit of his expertise. And to hell with bookkeeping and the car business, he thought.

So went Harry's days of retirement. Interesting. Fun. Diverting. Even if it was fantasy.

He had just begun researching his planned newsletter when something happened that would change Harry's life forever.

Arriving at the office one afternoon, the *Journal* and attaché case in hand, he found an envelope that had been deposited through the letter drop. It was plain, typewritten, addressed to whom? Never having received mail, he opened it immediately.

Thanking you in advance. Please contact me at your earliest convenience. I desperately need your help. Contact me at (703) 636-6336. Have answering service, will call you back immediately.
Laura N.

It was dated the previous day and signed with an ink pen. A bold signature. Harry turned the envelope over: To Whom, no return, no stamp. Just a sense of urgency and a phone number. Oh well, somebody mixing him up for somebody. And up the stairway he marched. He might need to invest in a more elaborate computer, he thought, what with the newsletter and everything.

Three days passed; a computer was ordered. Harry was so excited he thought this whole thing might become a reality. He was as wide eyed as the etching in the glass.

Entering the office he caught sight of the envelope as he stepped over it. He picked it up. It read: "H. Jones, Private Investigator." It dawned on him, for Christ's sake, some-body looking at the eye and the "private" on the door thought... He double-stepped the long stairway, walked out of his long coat, slouched into the big chair, and opened the envelope with a newly acquired, bone-handled letter opener. He read:

Dear Mr. Harry Jones. Urgent! I need you now! I will be at your office tomorrow at 1:00 p.m. for conference. If prior commitment, I'll wait. It is a private matter.
Laura N.

Same signature, same pen. Typewritten. The idea of a conference, leather chair to leather chair, eye to eye, seized him. Then reality caught up to him. Tapping a pencil on the desk, he said, "Jesus. Jesus Christ, I'll just tell her it's a mistake. The eye and all. Hell, I'm an investment guru!"

At one o'clock the worn stairs didn't so much as utter a creak. Harry knew by the draft that the door had opened. He was more nervous than he ever remembered. He only hoped the dim light of the room would help conceal his plight.

"Mr. Harry Jones?" she asked, knocking as she half-opened the door.

"Oh, yes. I didn't hear you. Pardon me. Please sit down."

Harry stood up, wheeled around the desk to offer the first of two chairs, pulling one out, ever so gentlemanly. He was proud of the office and the leather chairs. She seated herself in his chair, pulled it to the desk, laid her hands unclasped on the desk and, taking his pencil, with a tap, pointed for him to sit. Humbly, almost obediently, he seated himself in her chair.

"You didn't call me, " she said.

"This is a mistake."

"Maybe it was the Virginia number," she said, ignoring him. "Maybe I didn't give you a number. Did I?"

"You know this is a mistake."

"Did I tell you?" Pleading now. "Didn't I tell you my problem? Maybe...."

"I am not a detective. I am not a private eye," he stumbled, apologetically. "I am," he hesitated, then found the phrase, "an insurance investigator. Insurance fraud is my business. I handle insurance fraud cases." He peeked at her to see if it was working.

"I'm an insurance fraud," he fumbled. Then he blurted, "I'm a fraud investigator. Period."

He stopped, stood, turned away. Why the hell did I say that, he asked himself. What's wrong with stocks and bonds and the market letters, for Christ's sake?

She jumped to her feet, screaming. "But what's the difference? You're good at what you do. You're good. You've a reputation! You've been quoted. I've read the quotes." She paused, catching herself. He thought, amused, the only quotable remarks he'd ever made were in the *Washington Post* about car dealers and their selling schemes, and it wasn't even him, it was the car dealer who—

Interrupting his thought process, she said, "What difference does it matter what kind of investigator you are— you're an investigator!"

Without a tear she went straight for Harry, pointing for him to be seated. "Look, I have this problem." In perfect candor she told her story.

"I have a stepdaughter that has disappeared. She is twenty-eight, and her name is Karri." She handed him a snapshot. He noted a dark-haired young lady wearing sunglasses.

"I'll try to find one without the sunglasses," she continued. "My husband, her father, is sixty-six. Victor and I have been married eight years. If it's important, which it isn't—I'm thirty-eight." She was on the offensive.

"They are very close," she continued in a monotone. "Can I be more emphatic? She is uno number one in his life. Period. Number one. She's disappeared, and I need to find her." For want of more words, she massaged her neck with her left hand.

"He is completely distraught. I will introduce you to Victor if you wish."

She stood and turned her back to him. Studying the two Currier and Ives prints on the wall behind the desk, she continued, "I have persuaded my husband not to go to the police. Until we can investigate. If it's some protracted affair—it could be—Victor must be shielded from the embarrassment of publicity."

"It's been four weeks, with no contact," she added, thinking aloud. "That is not her mode of operation." She paused. "It is very quickly changing our lives. It has permeated everything in our lives. Do you understand?"

The lady tried to weep. By raising her hand to her chin

she caught herself, but said nothing. She looked at Harry for a response.

Harry looked at her and didn't know exactly what to say.

He thought he saw a tear run down her cheek as she slowly shook her head.

"And you haven't even ask my fucking name," she murmured.

The slip of the profanity invigorated Harry.

"You saw this eye on my door. You saw the word 'private'. You thought I was some sort of detective. I'm not, and I never will be—it's a mistake. I'm sorry. I'm sorry for your problem. But it's a mistake and I'm sorry."

Harry said no more. All of Harry's life he had been able to avoid the complications of mistakes—some real, some perceived, some his, some not—just by saying he was sorry. Admitting guilt. The quick way to end all unpleasantness. A shortcoming of Harry's; a failure recognized. But it worked! It ended things and life went on. Everyone who knew him—primarily Alice and his employers—knew this about Harry. It was accepted. On went life.

But now, for the first time in Harry's life, it wasn't working. Rising from behind the desk, with dramatically postured ease, she looked dead into his eyes and from three feet demanded, "You are going to find her for me, Harry Jones! You are going to find her, and I'm going to pay you handsomely. But you are going to find her. Tomorrow, at one o'clock, I will be back to present you with an advance of five thousand dollars. I will make arrangements for you to meet Victor if you like. He is very fragile, but I will make the arrangements. I will be back at one o'clock to offer you whatever information I might have. So that you can begin, Harry."

She turned, leaving him without a word to reply. As she closed the door, she looked back.

"My name is Laura, Harry."

"Yes," Harry said. "I was about to ask."

After she left he sat motionless for several minutes. He was emotionally exhausted. Shaking his head, trembling, he walked over to the armoire. He had stocked it with liquors as an offering to his clients. After discussing portfolios, it seemed appropriate. He removed a pint of peppermint schnapps. Of course it had not been opened. He snapped the lid and unscrewed it. Not being much of a drinker, he didn't know whether to expect a screw top or a cork. He filled a large, plain glass, not a period piece, and swallowed.

Harry walked back to his desk, tentatively, and sat down in his chair almost as if he didn't belong there. He set the glass down and closed his eyes. What in holy hell was going on, he wondered. And about her profanity, it seemed so out of character.

Profanity! Out of character! Let me get this straight, he thought. As he sipped he became more irritated. He thought about how he felt, sitting in his chair, in his office, at his leisure, and wondering if he belonged there. He loved the taste of the peppermint schnapps.

"I'll just be goddamned," he said aloud, sounding more like his ex-boss. "This lady walks into my office not knowing dick about me. She demands that I find her kid, who isn't even a kid, who isn't even hers, but her twice-as-old, old man's. Then she offers me five thousand bucks. *Five thousand*, for Christ's sakes. And here, me sitting here, in this fake office, faking as an insurance investigator when all the time I'm a fake financial consultant? All the while telling Alice Henrietta I'm studying my nonexistent investments? When all I ever wanted in the first place was to get the hell out of the house! Find something to do." Finishing the glass, emptying the pint bottle, shaking it out, he pondered his situation.

"What are you going to do, Mr. Harry? Now what are you going to do?"

After he thought and drank for several minutes, "I'll tell you what you're going to do, and I'll tell you what you are *not* going to do," he gathered his forces. "You are not going to fake it, number one. Fuck faking," he burped. "And you are not going to say you're sorry." With difficulty he attempted to pronounce each syllable aloud. He thought standing might help. He pushed the chair back, extending his arms, and braced himself against the desk, and stared down at the two chairs across from him.

Lecturing them, sarcastically, he said, "I'm sorry, Laura. I'm sorry, Alice Henrietta. I'm sorry, Mr. whoever my boss was."

"I'm sorry—bullshit!" he sneered menacingly into a decorative mirror. The warm peppermint schnapps tasted good to Harry. For an instant, he thought it was Christmas, not June. He remembered the first time he'd ever drunk schnapps with ice, at an office Christmas party. He peered through the empty hole in the bottle. He groped his way to the cabinet, priding himself on his insight. He knew his clients' preferences. Stocking an extra pint of schnapps was just one small example.

"Harry," he interrupted himself, "tell you what you're gonna do. You are about to become a detective, a *real* detective!" The last words were spoken emphatically, boosting an already over-zealous will. He would find the girl, and he would begin now by calling Laura and rescheduling the meeting for 9:00 a.m. sharp. There was a vigor about him. A nervousness he did feel, while also somewhat invigorated by the warm schnapps.

"Get this thing going," he muttered aloud. He fumbled in his desk top file for the first letter, the letter with the phone number. He checked the "in" file. Not being particularly cluttered with correspondence, he found it on top right where he had laid it. He dialed the 703 exchange and got a, "leave a number, will return the call," recording. Where was

703? He'd call information—better yet; check the area code index in the phone book. Harry's mind was clicking. Arlington, Virginia?

"What the hell's going on?" Harry muttered.

Late that afternoon after his return home and early retirement to bed, Alice Henrietta wondered aloud to her confidants. "I've never seen Harry like the Harry today. Never with so much spirit. Never with such confidence." Catching herself, feeling a need to minimize, she smiled, "He even asked me what *carpe diem* meant."

"Oh, that Harry," she mused.

9
:00 a.m. sharp.

"Drugs, Harry. Drugs are involved. At least I believe drugs. She has used them socially."

"Marijuana?"

"Yes."

"Cocaine?"

"Yes."

"Heroin?"

"Perhaps, socially. Socially, Harry," Laura emphasized.

"I mean how social can you get?"

"Maybe tried them all. I don't know... you're living in another era," she said, her voice rising. "You're either addicted or it's social."

She sounded to Harry like she knew the difference.

"I don't mean to say Karri's in rehab, seen a shrink. I just mean drugs could have an influence. Let me start with this. She's seeing a man named Jack Leach. A car dealer in Dewitt. Know the town?"

"I know the town," said Harry, dryly. He was taking notes.

"Some little guy. Some little town. I've never been introduced. She met him on a ski weekend. Fell for him. They meet on weekends. He's married. He's got something to do with this, Harry."

Laura took Harry's gaze into hers and repeated, with an air of authority, "It is the place to start."

"I may know the guy, Laura." He looked at her and was surprised at a rather blank, unresponsive stare. Maybe she was weary after all the pressures. From a girl she couldn't control and an aging husband she wanted to control. The pressures from a family Harry didn't even know. He was guessing.

"Fiftyish," Harry said, "Young looking. Athletic. Gold chain kind of guy," Harry liked his description. He smiled at her, breaking the tension. "Certainly the kind of guy I wouldn't like." She returned the smile. Harry didn't mention he'd met Leach at a dealer meeting, or that his ex-boss, a car dealer, knew Leach well. And Laura didn't ask how he knew Leach. Harry's mind wandered. He wondered how old he looked to her. The thought just passed through his mind.

"Incidentally," he asked, leaning back in his own chair, tapping his pencil on the arm, "where do you live?" He had not opened the envelope she had placed on his desk. By its bulk, he thought it was probably cash.

"Victor and I have an answering service in Arlington, Virginia," she said as if expecting the question. "Victor has large holdings there. However, we have a residence on Long Island... Quogue. Ever heard of it?"

"No."

"Near South Hampton. Quaint—you'd like it," she said, surveying his office. She stood up.

"I'll be going now, Harry. Stay in touch."

"I'll call you."

"If I think of anything else, I'll call. As things develop," she hesitated. "Well, we'll be in touch."

She smiled and left quietly. He could tell when she shut the outside door. The draft from the open window clicked the upstairs door to his office. She hadn't left him with much. He stood and went to the window. She was entering a taxi. As the driver held the door, her long, stocking legs hardly seemed capable of negotiating the small back seat. Not unlike a diver, about to spring into a forward double gainer, she gracefully unfolded in the car. For the first time Harry thought of her physique.

That night Harry and Alice Henrietta had their once-a-month tryst. It was usually little more. Things had never really gone very well in bed. Both had wed untried, and Harry had always shrugged it off, thinking that was the price you pay for a true, lasting relationship. Of course, he'd never known anyone well enough to ask about married sexual behavior. Alice, as customary, quickly went to sleep. However this night, in place of the usual frown, a slight wisp of a smile caressed her face. Those earlier thoughts about Harry's new spirit—they were partially confirmed.

Before a creature of habit, now Harry felt a need to change himself. He started abstractly with a list about himself. Stop patterning himself after himself. Start acting cautiously; inquiry meant questions, and questions meant suspicion. And suspicion, he knew, could ruin a plan. He needed to develop an air of caution about himself. And caution meant the way he used the phones, all the electronics he didn't understand. And no entries in the log, here. He could confide in no one; although, that seemed a moot challenge for Harry.

Harry had always thought of himself as fairly nondescript, but the dark suit he had worn every day, everywhere, forever—had to go. He would dress differently. Short sleeves, slacks, and loafers.

Alice's stare began at the floor, and it moved past his profile and backside as he dashed through the room in his new wardrobe. Her stare ended somewhere between the hanging glass and heaven. Yes, yes, she thought. What would retirement bring next?

Minutes later Harry returned to the room. The ladies dove for whatever projects were nearest.

"Signed up for flying lessons, girls, fly fishing, too. Out of your hair. Never had a hobby you know," Harry said, nodding to Alice.

"Yes, but don't you wear goggles and a parachute?" Alice quarried joyfully.

"Can't wear 'em over a suit, Alice!" They all laughed roundly, each much relieved in his or her own little way.

Harry contacted Darrell Davey by phone. They had met when Darrell was a district manager for Chrysler Corporation. Bonded by a mutual lack of business success, a friendship developed. Harry's lack of ambition and Darrell's unspectacular rise through corporate mediocrity brought each about what he wanted. They had even discussed buying a dealership together. Time eventually moved them apart. Yet they had been more than just business acquaintances. Car people, corporate and dealer, are tight-lipped concerning each other, making a veil of secrecy that is almost impregnable. This call was Harry's first challenge as a detective.

"I'm considering," Harry started, "just considering at this point, getting a small dealership. There's a small store in Dewitt, Jack Leach Chrysler. You familiar?"

"Yes, Harry. I was his D.M. Never aggressive. A run-down place. He didn't seem to care. Tell you, Harry, if you made the move, I'm positive the factory would support you. I'm excited that you're considering a dealership!"

"I'm just thinking. The area's good, isn't it?"

"It's not the area, Harry; it's growing like hell. It's just Jack Leach. Certain things stick out about dealers. It was strange. When we'd get something really hot, like the minivans and pickups, dealers would beg for allocation. You know, everybody fought for anything extra. Begged, pleaded, for Christ's sake. Jack Leach never asked for a thing. Never any stories, no demands, no going-over-the-head threats. Nothing."

"How has he lasted so long?" Harry asked.

"Hell, I don't know. The factory would have terminated him if they could. But he sold his minimums—had a good customer satisfaction rating. I'll tell you, Harry, the factory would be very excited with a deal. He aggravates the hell out of them."

"How's that?"

"Low volume. The fact he's gone a lot. In the summer I couldn't talk to him. Jack was a boating nut. Suppose he still is… the business is there, Harry."

"A boating nut," Harry repeated.

"Oh, Jesus, sailing was his thing. Pictures of sailboats all over the dealership. Half-hulls on the walls, models in glass cases, you'd think he ran a boat sales instead of a car lot. Had a big boat. Gone a week, two weeks a month. Never there when I'd call on him. Nobody to make a god-damned decision.

"Talk to 'em, Harry. I tell you, I know we'd be on board with this one. Want me to set something up?" Darrell asked.

"No, no," Harry interrupted. "This is strictly on the Q.T. I want to nose around a little. Strictly on the Q.T. for now."

"Fine. I'm with you, buddy. Call me anytime." Darrell ended the conversation. He called Harry back within the hour. Jack was still in the boat business. Big time! Had a new forty-five foot sailboat. Laughingly, he told Harry he would find Leach in Frankfort where he kept the boat.

"How Jack can afford that size boat on what his dealership makes," Darrell added, "I'll never know."

Harry thought this might be a little easier than expected. A forty-five foot boat. Never at the dealership. He reminded himself that his job was only to find the girl, period. Find the girl. Call his client. Case number one closed. Bingo! He couldn't wait to call Laura.

Driving north he thought about drugs. The dependency. It was kind of simple, Harry thought. You took them to feel better, and you had to keep taking them to continue feeling better, and pretty soon you took so many of them to continually feel great that they finally ruined your health. He'd heard the bad stories, but never had a feeling about them, philosophical or real. He had never used them, and to the best of his knowledge, never known anyone who had. He'd read where in the early part of the century drugs—heroin and cocaine—were considered a rich man's pastime. And nothing ever seemed to work up from the poor; it was always down from the rich. Crack cocaine was everyman's drug. He thought it was the reason for most crime and he knew anything worth twenty-five dollars was fair game for those using crack—car radios, VCR's, cheap guns, anything. What was once a private recreation was now a public disaster. The rich probably did it better, he reluctantly concluded. Maybe the rich mentality could handle things like that better than the poor.

Harry thought about Laura. What was her interest? He didn't think it was just the well-being of her stepdaughter. He concluded his client's motives were no more of his concern than if he were her lawyer. He was being paid to do a job.

He drove by Dewitt on his way to Frankfort. Approaching the square, yellow-brick World War II building, the dealership, there was an impertinence about the place that Harry considered almost comical. He didn't see the disciplined look of a car dealership; the straight lines of cars and trucks, the separation between new and used, not even the cosmetics—the banners and flags and window murals. The floodlights hung from cresol stained telephone poles. On an empty lot across the street the overly large outdated penstar sign stood like an afterthought. People liked the sign. The Dewitt farmers, the rural folks, and the city people moving to the suburbs probably thought it quaint. He knew that Chrysler had replaced those signs years ago. He guessed their interest in Jack Leach had long since waned, and he wondered how long he'd been there and how long he would last.

He shrugged it off. It was just that the Jack Leach he'd seen at a dealer function didn't square with his business. Darrell was right. Harry was sure Chrysler would like a change. Was there a twinkle in Harry's eye? Hell, no, he thought. That was the last thing he needed to screw up his retirement. His new occupation was just fine.

There were three marinas in Frankfort, a coastal village cut between the mountainously high sand dunes that swept along the northwestern shoreline of Michigan. Towns like Frankfort existed where rivers flowing westward spilled into Lake Michigan. A hundred years ago they were fishing villages and ports for the logging industry. Now they were resort towns, havens for the sport fishermen, weekenders for the working hordes of southern Michigan, and marinas for the affluent of the Midwest.

Some of the towns exist only as ghost towns. Others, those surviving, were hardly known even by down-staters. They had names like Good Heart, Cross Village, Leland, and Manistee. Villages like Arcadia, Grand Marais, Pentwater, Empire, Glen Haven, and Glen Arbor. Names, themselves, that seemed to tell something about the people who had called them home—lumber barons, fishermen, sea captains, and the native Indians.

He found Jack Leach's boat at one of the two private marinas, a discreetly attired yacht club with uniformed dockhands dressed in white shirts and black slacks. He walked down the peer, past slip twenty-one. Two men were cleaning teak and polishing brass. They were enjoying their work. Harry walked to the end, surveyed the becalmed harbor, and watched the people. Some were busying themselves with trifles; most were lounging, doing nothing important nor wanting to do anything important. Not particularly friendly people, these yachtsmen, Harry thought; not interested in small talk. Probably just damned glad to be away from other people. Kind of the way Harry felt about people, even without a boat.

Harry strolled back up the pier past the two young men who were cleaning the shiny, black-hulled sailboat. He turned back. He didn't know what a classic boat should look like, but if anything was classic, this was.

A white sailboat, about the same size, was moored next to it with a "for sale" sign taped to the mast.

"What would a boat like this cost?" he asked the two dock hands, who now looked up at him.

"They're asking eighty thousand."

"Lot of money. Lot of boat, though," Harry added, in defense of his ignorance.

"Think that's a lot? This girl's about five times that," one said, referring to the black-hulled sailboat.

"Wouldn't you say four-hundred thousand?" asked the other.

"Yup, this is a Hinckley."

"Hinckley?" Harry asked.

"Sou'wester forty-two," A reverence broke into the conversation. "She's custom built. Only two a year. Built in Maine."

"A long wait for one of these?"

"Good four to five years."

"You've really got to like boats," Harry groping for conversation.

"Was a hell of a boat Mr. Leach had before. Would've made most anyone I know awful happy."

"Heart light III," the other added, as if being a part of something important. "This is number four."

"What makes one eighty, and the other four hundred and eighty?" Harry asked. "Look pretty much the same size, pretty much the same to me."

"Come aboard, I'll show you," one said, not hesitating. "Mr. Leach won't be here till the weekend. He wouldn't like this, but what the hell. 'Never let anyone aboard,' he says."

The interior of the boat was all highly varnished wood, the brightwork so brilliant that it made Harry squint. A showpiece that looked just launched. Harry saw no sign that anyone was living aboard.

"See this—cherrywood. Eight coats of varnish." It didn't look like wood to Harry.

"Here," he said, leading Harry forward. "The sink tops are all marble. It's all custom. You tell 'em how you want it. That's how they build her."

He then started to praise the Hinckley's powerful aft section, its fine entry, its air-foiled section keel, its reduced wetted surface, none of which Harry understood. Harry interrupted, "How many does it take to operate a boat like this?"

"In Mr. Leach's case, one."

"One person can handle this—alone?"

"He single-hands it all the time. Comes on a Friday

night, sails a week, brings her back to us. Sometimes twice a month, maybe more."

"Never anyone else," Harry said, shaking his head, as if in disbelief.

"Wife, kids, once a summer."

"Hell, the guy oughta at least have a girl friend," Harry said. They all laughed.

"Not Mr. Leach. Nope he's a real loner—a *real* sailor."

Shaking hands, thanking them, Harry started to leave. He thought of one thing.

"If a guy were to have a boat up here, where'd he sail? Say for a weekend, say five days," he added, eyeing the white boat with the "for sale" sign.

"I'd sail up to Leland. 'Round the Manitou Islands," one suggested. "Beyond the Sleeping Bear...."

"I'd sail over to Door County," said the other. "Great scenery, remote."

"Sail up to the Beavers."

"Yeah, there's a place! Beaver Island. Remote."

"That's where this lady goes."

"And one guy can do it?" Harry asked.

"Follow Mr. Leach sometime." They laughed and waved goodbye.

"Thanks," Harry said. "Someday I might do that."

Sitting in an outdoor restaurant, gazing at the marina and harbor, sipping ice tea, two things crossed Harry's wrinkled brow. How could Jack Leach afford that boat, and where the hell was Karri? She sure as the devil wasn't being kept on that boat. He watched the two men moving about the boat, thinking he's done quite well, but doubting his earlier prediction of a quick end to everything here in Frankfort.

He wasn't daunted by the prospect of a lengthier, more involved search. Not in the least. In fact he felt good that it hadn't been that easy and that it wasn't over. Leaving town, he stopped at the city marina. The attendant was not busy. He looked like a real sailor.

"If you sailed up to Beaver Island," Harry inquired, "would you sail straight through?"

"Probably. It's a good twelve hours—rhumb line. If the wind's right. Most people sail to Leland, though. Nice day-sail. Spend the night, then a good sail to Beaver. You sailing up?"

"Maybe."

"St. James Harbor's on the northeast side. If you've never been there, you'll like it. Well protected from the weather. Remote. People leave you alone. No high rollers out there."

"Are there year-round people?"

"Maybe three hundred fifty. Ten times that in the summer. Ferry runs from Charlevoix every day, sometimes twice."

On Saturday morning Jack Leach backed out of the mooring. He had arrived sometime during the night, Harry didn't know when, but he was alone. A dockhand threw Leach the lines and waved. Jack was too busy to be personable. Harry felt a tinge of jealousy. It was not the sailboat. It was the independence and self-assuredness that seemed to go along with Jack Leach and his pastime.

Winding his way up the coast to Leland, Harry again wondered how he'd lived his life in Michigan and never seen these places. Leland was smaller than Frankfort. It was a harbor of refuge, man-made, with jetties of huge, cut limestone rock. Summer cottages and shops were pinched closely to the harbor, which was large enough for only a few visiting boats.

Other than several charter boats for the salmon fishing, there was no permanent dockage. The village owned the marina. Everyone sailing in and out was a transient. It was, however, large enough for a few big boats. This would be the place to keep a lover, Harry thought. A place where someone could be content to live, quietly consenting to a second life.

It took three hours to drive there, and by Harry's calculations, another three for the sailboat to arrive. By early afternoon there was no dark-hulled boat on the horizon. Through his binoculars, the harbormaster could make out a large sailboat moving north, staying well out, perhaps eight miles off shore. The harbormaster, Charlie, reckoned by the wind speed that if she were going to Beaver Island it would be well after dark; ten, closer to eleven o'clock. Did he want Charlie to raise the boat on the VHF? No, Harry said he'd see him on the island. They were just acquaintances.

After giving enough time, Harry left Leland for Charlevoix and the ferry. Maybe Leach's destination was Beaver Island for a week, maybe two weeks, a month? An island sounded a little remote, yet Harry admitted to himself he didn't know how people thought, what they did, how these liaisons were carried out. He felt some doubt and would liked to have called Laura. Just to confirm things. Laura had been sure Karri was with Jack Leach. No question. He was beginning to see a pattern with Jack, but nothing about Karri was showing up. He couldn't forget Laura's demands; "You are going to find her for me, Harry Jones. You are going to find her. I'm going to pay you well. But *you* are going to find her!" She seemed so sure about Jack Leach. Maybe her stepdaughter was some flighty broad with two or three Jack Leach's. He would call Laura that night from the hotel on Beaver Island.

When he made arrangements, the eight-room Erin Hotel had six vacancies. Once there, he met the other occupant, a surveyor from St. Ignace named Will. His room overlooked the ferry dock and the marina. The marina had a small shanty of an office at the end of the main dock. A weathered, half-broken sign with "Harbor Master" hung above the door. The door was locked, the wind was blowing, and a notice on the door said, "Prudent sailors always have fair winds."

Harry called Laura. He left his number. She returned his call late that evening. She sounded hesitant and said she didn't want to review things over the phone, but, yes, she had heard from Karri, who had seemed vaguely coherent, would not disclose her whereabouts, and babbled on and on about Jack Leach. Everything was about Jack Leach.

"Yes, Harry, you've got the direction. I'm so pleased with you. In a week, maybe two, we'll meet and review. Or, call if you have news," she added, as if an afterthought. Then she hung up the phone.

Harry felt better that evening. He walked back to the municipal marina and met the harbormaster, a congenial fellow who gave him a brief history of the island. He told how the Irish Catholics settled it during the time of the potato famine, and how they were run off by the Mormons who set up a kingdom on the island, followed by intrigue and murder, the flight of the Mormons, and the return of the Irish to resettle it as it now existed.

He walked from one end of the town to the other. A distance of a few hundred yards. It circled St. James Harbor. The harbor was naturally protected, with a wide entrance to the southeast. On a good day you could look east and see the mainland twenty-five miles away. A lighthouse guarded the entrance.

A fishing trawler turned inward from the lake beyond the lighthouse toward the protection of the harbor. Gulls spiraled upward, screaming, diving beyond the stern of the boat as they welcomed its return. The rapid cur-jung, cur-jung of its engines, soft and almost powerless, would become a familiar sound to Harry. There were four fishing boats on the island, although to

Harry they looked more like railroad cars than boats. Indians owned all of them. The Indians were the only ones who could fish commercially on the Great Lakes, a right deeded to them by an old treaty. Two tugs with barges loaded with lumber hugged the shore. Both flew the flag of Ireland. The island, shaped like Ireland, was still predominately Irish Catholic. Harry counted the small commercial establishments on one hand, not including the single-story power plant. The hotel was the tallest building on the island. It was two stories high.

To Harry's surprise, the sailboat did not come in that night. At least not before midnight. He walked across the street from the hotel to the Shamrock bar and ordered a schnapps. The harbormaster was sitting at the bar, explaining a joke to the barkeeper. His laugh was better than the joke; it started like an engine with a worn battery, slowly turning, coughing, grabbing, then whirling like it was finally hitting on all eight.

"Ya know how you talk to a fish," he asked in a monotone. "Ya drop him a line."

The four men sitting at the bar laughed at his laugh. The joke, like the island, was a half-century in the past. The barkeeper wasn't amused. One long sweep of the bar with his cleaning rag, and he moved away; he'd heard it before.

The boat wasn't there in the morning either. Harry was confused. Was the sailor in Frankfort wrong about sailing time to Leland? Had he miscalculated and left for Charlevoix too early? He called the marina in Leland, and Charlie said no Heartlight registered last night; no Hinckley Sou'wester in his harbor. Two boats came into St. James during the day. Both power boats, one from the east, Mackinac Island, the other from the south. Neither had seen a black-hulled sailboat.

Later that afternoon, sitting in the Shamrock, Harry struck up a conversation with one of the Indian fisherman. He had gone out early and come in early. The fishing was bad; besides, it was Sunday. A good day to be alone in the bar. Harry assumed it to be a social event, sitting in the bar alone and drinking beer. No, the Indian did not see much recreational-type boat traffic this far out in the lake. The Indian shook his head, and Harry knew the questions would have to be shorter and more to the point. No, there weren't many sport fishermen out here; thank you, Mary Mother of Jesus. No, nobody lived on the other islands. He informed Harry there were eight islands in the chain. Chain—the word archipelago confused him, made him restless. But the Indian was coming around.

Harry bought a round. A schnapps for himself, a draft for his friend. Yes, the Indian had lived all his life on the island. He liked most all the people. There were three types on the island; natives, transplants, and summer people. The natives and summer people he mostly liked. The transplants—hardly. Most of the transplants were there because they didn't fit anyplace else. What did the transplants do for a living? They worked for contractors building summer cottages. They cut timber. They drew welfare, food stamps. He worked; he fished for a living. Like his father and grandfather before him. He had two helpers—one Indian, one a transplant. The transplant wasn't worth a damn, sometimes didn't get up early and come to work. The Indian and Harry had another round. Harry bought. Transplants were lazy. Would rather live off the government. Smoke pot and collect welfare. If he'd lived that way his mother would have killed him. Had two brothers, both dead. One was killed in Vietnam, the other drowned fishing. Both buried on the island, though, in the back of the cemetery where all Indians were buried. Harry could see for himself. Mother never got over it. Never got over seeing father and grandfather die, either. Never liked the idea of living on an Indian reservation. Did Harry know his house on Beaver Island was a reservation? Didn't know his name was John, either. Knew John was a worker, though. Proud to drink with an Indian fisherman named John, and sorry he had to put up with a lazy, pot smoking, drunk transplant. Deserved a lot better. Deserved good fishing and good luck. The Indian, having had a look of despondency about him, now seemed rejuvenated.

"Fishermen have a good life," John toasted. "To good friends, good drinks, good talks." Hoisting his glass, Harry nodded sheepishly. The bartender looked up at John and Harry. Kind of like the look when Alice Henrietta first saw Harry in his new wardrobe.

Harry's room faced dead east. Staring through the glare of the coastal sunrise, the first thing to catch his attention was the sailboat. He made coffee and sat on the edge of the bed. More coffee, then the chair. For an hour he watched the boat through his hangover. It appeared to be unattended. He was curious. Leach could be sleeping, waiting for Karri to arrive by ferry. Harry took a long, head-clearing walk that ended at the harbormaster's shack. He found the harbormaster straining over his logbook. His friendship with the harbormaster had blossomed early. His name was Glenallen, and his favorite drink at the Shamrock was schnapps with a beer chaser.

"Now, that is a beauty," Harry said, pointing to the boat.

"Yep."

"First time in?"

"Nope."

In the morning short answers were commonplace on Beaver Island. The Shamrock shouldered most of the blame.

"See her often?"

"Every couple of weeks…. Stays a couple days. Leaves. Has a place on the island."

"Jesus, a boat like that and doesn't stay on it?"

"Creature of habit. Sails up from Frankfort. Anchors off North Fox for a day or two. Stays at his place a couple days. Leaves…."

"What's North Fox?"

"An island, eleven miles south."

Glenallen shrugged his shoulders, picked his teeth, and continued working on his books. Harry thought he could have helped with the accounting, but didn't offer.

"John says it scares him… taking a boat like that into North Fox, so close on the south side. Boulders big as houses. And anchoring in there…." Glenallen leaned back in his chair.

"Beautiful island, though. No one lives out there. Really have to know the place. And anchoring off the south side, no one goes over there."

"John knows it?" Harry asked.

"John fishes between North and South Fox."

J ack Leach's cottage was a New England salt-box, sided with cedar shake, built well back along the high, tertiary dunes on the southernmost tip of Beaver Island. An area known as Cheyenne Point. So remote that few summer places were built along this windswept part of the island. It was eleven miles from St. James Harbor, a long drive through a birch forest of back roads. It was hardly noticeable among the sand dunes, but you could not see it from the road, only a path you wouldn't otherwise know existed.

Harry had borrowed a pickup from Glenallen for ten dollars. Parking near a closed cottage, he walked straight to the beach, then down toward Jack Leach's cottage. As he walked the beach, he prodded with a large stick, appearing to pay no attention to the man standing alone on the porch above and fifty yards from him. The man was heavily tanned with sun-bleached hair and a cropped beard. Drinking from a coffee mug, he had a hyperactiveness about his movements. It was Jack Leach. Harry continued down the beach, poking and prodding.

Several hundred yards and beyond sight of an abandoned lighthouse, he turned and started back. The figure was gone. Connected to Leach's cottage was a high, tower-like stairwell. It was also covered with cedar-shake. A neatly designed place, Harry thought, architecturally suited for the land and the high woods well behind it. Harry noticed a large telescope in a tower window. It was directed toward the southwest, toward North Fox Island. Harry walked past, and Jack Leach did not reappear. Nor did anyone else. Harry would return later after Leach had sailed from the island.

Jack Leach stayed on the island for two days. He didn't meet anyone at the ferry and, to the best of Harry's knowledge, no one flew in on the charter flying service to meet him. Harry kept an eye out for a red Jeep that Jack kept on the island, and he never saw either Jack or the Jeep at the Shamrock. Harry discovered a lodge on the north side of the island, facing Garden, Squaw, and Whiskey Islands, and the second night he saw the Jeep and thought Jack was probably there having dinner.

When Harry returned, the cottage was empty. Peering through the sliding-glass doors, it reminded him of the boat: too well maintained. Not actually alive, almost antiseptic. Harry was told about summer people. How they kept their shades undrawn for open viewing, to discourage theft, but the place should have looked more casual; books, magazines, an ottoman. Nothing. Like a hotel suite, he thought. For so much outward character, it needed a decorator.

Harry hadn't asked anyone if Jack Leach had a companion. Before he arrived, he expected Karri to be there. Again Harry was confused. Things should have begun to fall into place. Everything seemed logical enough to be leading to a solution that wasn't there. At least to this point. Where would she be? And what about this cottage, a half-million plus? He looked again at the window in the tower and the telescope aimed at North Fox Island. The island, encased in a morning haze, seemed further than eleven miles from Beaver.

Harry asked Glenallen about renting a boat, a small boat with a motor so he could go fishing alone. Glenallen knew someone. What about twenty-five a day, plus gas, even throw in the fishing gear? Harry agreed. Bait and license at the hardware. Glenallen warned him about the temperament of "The Big Lake," as he called it. If you go out of the bay, he warned, stay in close. And watch the boulders. They were in the middle of a good high, he explained, and the Big Lake should stay flat for a couple more days.

Harry phoned Alice. She was excited about his upcoming fishing experience, as she called it. The lake worried her, but she wished him good luck.

Darrell was in when Harry called.

"On the Q.T., what does Leach make a year?"

"I'm guessing—wait, let me get it up." There was a pause.

"Forty-eight thousand, six hundred year-to-date. That's a damned crime," he said. "Should make five times that."

"Isn't it ...?" Returned Harry.

The next morning Harry went fishing. Even with the extra ten gallons of fuel and the auxiliary electric motor, he was worried. He motored close to shore. Once around the south end of the island, he increased speed so that the boat would plane. With the lake flat and a clear sky, the distance between Beaver Island and North Fox Island vanished surprisingly fast.

North Fox Island was little more than a mile long, east to west, a half mile north to south. The north side, facing Beaver Island, was wooded to the water's edge; the south side was sand dunes with white beach running the length. If not for the conifers, it could well have been a south sea poster island, Harry thought. And, if not for the forty-five degree temperature of the water. He surmised a guy would die of hypothermia within a half hour in this water.

There was one cottage on the island. He pulled the boat well up onto the sandy beach and scrambled up what was left of stairs leading to the cottage. Years of pounding surf and wind had covered much of the wooden steps with sand. It was more of a house than a cottage. A high, impressive "V" of a porch, made of solid cement, jutted from the hill overlooking the beach. A ten-foot inside fireplace with an eight-foot opening dominated the small interior, which was mostly a glassed-in living room. It could have been a Frank Lloyd Wright creation, Harry thought, entering through an unlocked main door. There wasn't much sign of life, other than a note above the toilet stool, pleading "for whom" to fill with a bucket of water before using. Cupboards were open, mice droppings everywhere, magazines dated years earlier, bare mattresses and the mildewed smell of neglect. It wasn't part of this story, he thought, but it was part of somebody's story.

There was a car path, hardly a road, leading west from the house into the woods. Harry followed it. It was overgrown and had not been traveled recently by any motorized vehicles, only used as a footpath. The trees were tall hard-woods, mostly oaks with some birch. The undergrowth was thick so that the real light came only as rays from above. Harry followed the path over fallen trees and thickly over-grown streams, bridged only by rotting, moss-covered, hand-hewn timbers. Through bogs and lifeless ponds, Harry was on an adventure, almost forgetting his purpose.

Abruptly, the path rose to a shed and beyond to a clear-ing so large that it startled Harry. Surrounded by forest, he walked into the opening. It had been cleared as deep as the island, itself. At least a half-mile in length. A good eighty yards wide, it was mowed to the ground, and surprisingly well groomed. This was a goddamned airfield! Right in the middle of nowhere in the middle of Lake Michigan. Harry wheeled, suddenly feeling not alone. Standing there in the opening he felt vulnerable. He wished he were back in the woods. It frightened him. He fought for a sound, any sound, but there was nothing; only the caw of crows in distant trees. He waited for his nerves to calm. At least enough to move. Finally, quietly he edged back into the trees and sat down. It took Harry about as long to recover as it had to fix the hangover the previous morning. Chilled, he stood up, realizing it was just he and this island and the fishing boat. He opened the door to the big Quonset hut. Inside was an old Jeep, a brush hog, and a hundred smudge pots. The Jeep started, the pots were full of oil, and Harry got the hell out of the place.

He was done with North Fox Island. At least for now.

Still flushed when he returned the boat to the dock, he walked straight for the Shamrock. Glenallen came in the bar sometime later.

"The fish, Harry? Want to explain the big one that got away?" Schnapps guys get personal real easy.

Harry asked, his tension easing, "Those people with summer cottages, do they ever come up in the winter? For

Christmas... the holidays... fly up?"

"Some do."

"The guy with the black boat?"

This was the first time Harry felt that he had over-stepped a boundary of inquisitiveness. But he felt he needed to do it, and he knew what he was doing.

"Never," Glenallen answered.

"Hell," the harbormaster said, after a pause. "Told me he's thinking about trucking her to Florida. Got a place in Naples. Jesus fucking Christ, can you imagine what *that* place must be like?"

"Can't imagine."

"You ever thought, Harry, just once in your life having all that shit?"

"Not until just now."

D riving home from Charlevoix, Harry decided to check the Jack Leach home in Dewitt. He was sure he wasn't going to be surprised if he found a conservative place in a nice middle-income neighborhood. In a small subdivision, on a cul-de-sac. He wasn't surprised at all.

A vengefulness set upon Harry Jones. He called Jack Leach Chrysler every day. He was always someone differ-ent—the local paper-classified ads, the police athletic league for donations, the Chrysler zone office for the boss, the Chamber of Commerce.

Finally on the eighth day:

"Mr. Leach will be out of the office for a few days," the office manager said curtly.

"Jack's gone sailing," a salesman said.

"Come five, he's out-a-here, bye-bye," the parts guy said, not caring who or why.

Harry packed, explaining to the girls he'd been bitten by the fishing bug. He kissed Alice Henrietta, told her he'd be back in three or four days, would call, and left.

He flew from the Charlevoix airport to Beaver Island and stayed in the same room at the Erin Hotel. He made arrangements for the boat. Except for an exchange with Glenallen about getting the bug, he saved his nerves for himself. He sat in his room looking out at the bay, planning his rendezvous. He was glad Laura had not called. He knew this was bigger than Laura and Karri. He was sure Karri would pop up somewhere. It was inevitable in the scheme of things. Maybe she was not even an innocent victim. But that was another story. Right now, if the conclusions he had drawn proved correct, this was enormous. When he finally disclosed what was going on up here, Harry knew he would be making much more than just a satisfying retirement out of his life. He would be making a life out of his retirement.

He stared out into the darkness of the bay, ringed now with soft lights of the houses and an occasional streetlight. He looked down at his hands, and they were shaking.

A morning breeze blew out of the southeast causing a slight chop. Later, as the day warmed, it would flatten out. Nothing to worry about, Glenallen assured him. Harry said if the fishing were good, he might stay out all night in the bay. Not to worry, he'd stay in close.

"No fish stories," the harbormaster waved, as Harry left the dock.

He motored directly into the tree-covered, north side of North Fox Island, putting the boat close to the trees. He sat on the back of the boat, casting his bait into the cold water. He didn't believe anyone was on the island yet, but if they were, he wanted them to notice him and confront him early. After eating sandwiches, and not being seen, heard, or approached by anyone, he pulled the boat into the trees and hiked inland. Creeping, he moved to the far edge of the tree line, opposite the shack. Lying flat, he estimated his distance at one hundred yards. A good distance. Steadying the binoculars, he brought the "no smoking" sign on the door dangerously close to him. He was satisfied. In the proper light he would be able to identify faces. Then, he and his nerves waited. Time went slowly. He thought of a Gordon Lightfoot song, "Does anyone know where the love of God goes, when the waves turn the minutes to hours." A good song. Not appropriate here, he thought, but a good song.

He thought about Laura. If he proved himself right, and Karri became a bit player, how would Laura react? Would it be an ego thing? At some point this would become an honesty problem between Laura and him. He would tell her about this before anyone else. She could help him set the priorities or reset them. Then, what would her priorities be? After all, she was doing all this for her own sake, for her marriage, not particularly for Karri's well being. Or could this become a life or death situation for Karri? He must find her. After all, it was his job. She was somewhere soaking it up, probably in Naples. Hell, he thought impulsively, where the hell would she rather be, out on some sailboat, on some island with a bunch of drunks, or in Naples, Florida? Chalk one up for Naples... and he'd never even been there. Leland? Well, maybe in the summer.

Harry made up his mind; he'd travel to Naples the following week. That has got to be it, he thought. How many places can Jack Leach own? Didn't the Internal Revenue

Service track things like that? He doubted it. In the scheme of things, he guessed the I.R.S. had bigger problems to worry about. But priorities? He thought not. What is worse, some guy stealing a million bucks in business or some guy being the catalyst for a thousand wasted lives, murders, genetic failures?

At about the point where Harry was becoming philosophical, crows screamed, springing from distant trees in the forest beyond the shack. There was movement in the woods. A man appeared carrying what looked to Harry like weighted mail satchels. He knew, without steadying the glasses, that it was Jack Leach throwing the bags to the ground and returning to the woods. Thirty minutes later the same: crows forewarning, two bags tossed to the ground and an exit. With the heat of the early afternoon and the weight of the bags, the time lengthened between each trip. Finally it stopped. Harry hadn't counted the trips. If it were drugs, cocaine, and he knew it was, it had come a long way from the hills and valleys of Columbia, Bolivia, or Peru to this uninhabited island in upper Lake Michigan. And its journey of destruction had only begun.

Jack Leach sat on the bags and mopped his brow and drank from a bagged container. Harry's sweat made it difficult to focus the glasses. He thought, here was a guy, probably worth millions, sweating his ass off and brown bagging it like a wino. Resting his head on the bags, tilting a cap over his eyes, Jack Leach rested. Harry, shaking like he had a bad case of the chills, waited him out.

Toward nightfall Harry heard the plane. It circled twice. Jack Leach stood up, brushed off his pants, looked straight at the trees where Harry was hiding, and relieved himself. The twin-engine plane came in low over the trees from the north, landed smoothly, and taxied up to where Jack was waiting. Its engines continued to run at idle. A door opened, and two Dobermans jumped from the plane. Harry was suddenly scared sick. His stomach turned his mouth bitter. He lost focus then caught it. The dogs circled the plane, widening their circumference at each turn. Their actions were almost mechanical. Should he crawl back slowly, then make a run for the boat? He wouldn't make it. He caught himself again just as the dogs took Leach's scent and bounded into the woods beyond the shack. The men were loading the plane hurriedly.

Harry looked up into the trees. There was still a slight breeze from the southeast. That should help—keeping his scent from reaching the dogs. Was that rational? Yes, maybe. The sound of the engines might help him, banging through the trees if he ran. What about the dogs? Could he fight them off? He began to feel sick again. Don't puke, goddamn you, he muttered. Don't puke. He frantically put the glasses in focus. Steady as possible. The two men were small in stature. One looked a little like Jack, the other was short, dark, high cheekbones.

Just as he slipped with a thought about none of the three looking particularly menacing, the Doberman Pinschers dashed from the trees, sprung, and with a midair twisting dance, bolted, head down, straight for Harry. Scared, gutless, he froze to the ground. Spread-eagle, he'd be taken. He knew it. As he dug his head into the matted leaves, he suddenly heard a high-pitched whistle. Then two more. He peeked. The dogs, not twenty yards away, whirled; confused, disoriented, they seemed to run straight down the runway in the direction from which the plane had landed. Then stopped. Two more whistles and they dashed for the plane. The last bags were loaded; the two men were hustling to leave. The doors slammed shut. The engines revved. What transpired in those last several minutes, Harry had no idea. The plane quickly taxied to the north end of the runway, and, in one motion, turned and started, full throttle, down the runway toward him. The plane lifted beyond the trees and the island. Jack Leach had already disappeared.

Harry lay there for two hours, motionless. He didn't move a bone in his body. He didn't so much as blink an eyelid. He wasn't hungry, he was not thirsty. He couldn't pee if he wanted. He was aware of no functioning body parts except his heart. His hands were numb, as were his legs, arms, even his peter. As his father would have said, he was dead from the ass both ways. His mind was not, however. Oh, no, his mind was working just fine; you goddamned dumb silly son-of-a-bitch! Whatever in the holy fuck are you doing here?

First crawling, then creeping, stumbling, and staggering through the woods, he made it to the shore. Surprisingly, he came out right where he had entered. It was a still night, and he was glad he had the electric trolling motor with him. It ran quietly in the calm water, and he used it until the battery went dead. Then he started the bigger engine and headed for St. James. The lighthouse, blinking red, at the entrance to the harbor was a welcomed return sight. Not as welcome as the Shamrock, though.

"No stories, Harry?" Glenallen greeted him.

"No stories."

He wasn't surprised at the gaunt look he saw in the saloon mirror.

A day later, a more relaxed Harry Jones wondered at what point authorities should be notified. Laura would be consulted first. After he came back from Florida. She was his employer, after all, and his job for her had not been completed. He wanted that part done. Telling her the whole story would be the coup.

Harry Jones, however, was being driven by both his curiosity and a developing hatred for Jack Leach. He needed to know more about this drug business. Where were these drugs coming from and where were they going? It would be easy to find where it ended up, he thought. The law could do that.

In Harry's mind, the important question still remaining was how did Leach get the drugs. How did these satchels get into his hands so that he could make this connection work? And why Jack Leach? Why was he a fixture in all this? When the time came for Harry to turn all this over to the right people, he knew this would be a link that needed closing. Someone would solve this, and he was sure he could find the answers himself. He wanted to know. Maybe he was just that close. Feeling somewhat immune from the danger, he was determined to find out how Jack Leach got the drugs.

As he flew to Florida, Harry formed a plan. He needed access to Leach's dealership. He knew that car dealers trade cars among themselves. One dealer has the customer; another dealer has the car with the right color, the right accessories. So they swap. Or sometimes they trade just to give their inventory a new look. They need people to drive the cars, and they use drivers "off the street," not on the payroll, no deductions, just fifteen or twenty bucks under the table—one of those gray-market things. Harry would become a driver. He would walk into Jack Leach Chrysler, tell the sales-manager he was retired, that he could use the money, would be reliable, and had a good driving record. He would explain that he didn't have a phone, but he'd call every day. Harry knew he could be at the dealership in forty minutes. It wasn't convenient, but it was an opening. At thirty thousand feet, over a schnapps, he felt a little smug. His ingenuity appalled him.

Naples. The bistro of Naples. Sitting at a window table in an exclusive restaurant at noon in Naples, Harry knew this was a money town. He felt out of sync. As Harry saw it, the eatery, as well as the town's quaint shopping mall was a mid-day, tailored, sports jacket with mismatched, pleated slacks. The men, his age or slightly older, were all silver haired and deeply tanned, all with gorgeous women carrying large packages, running everywhere and going nowhere. The extravagance of everything! When a waiter brought Harry's salad fork in a bowl of ice, then removed it and laid it on his salad dish, and removed the bowl with a bow, Harry knew he was out of his league. He was having second thoughts about his wardrobe; his short-sleeved, Hawaiian sports shirt and baggy pants. He sat alone and observed.

The two-story condominium directly across from him, in the bay, surrounded by water, had eight apartments, four on each floor, all with corner views. Connecting the building with the palm-shaded street was a gated driveway, thirty feet long, about the same distance above the water, which led to the garage area below the apartments. It was well secured. Harry figured the apartments had to be three-quarters of a million. This whole thing made Harry uneasy.

He took notes on the tight security at Jack Leach's condominium. He knew which one was Leach's and was determined to get inside. Driving to Charlevoix, taking a ten-minute flight and a room at the Erin was one thing, but flying to Naples, Florida, another. There was no plan to return empty-handed. He noticed that everyone who entered either had a magnetic card, a key, or a password. Harry had none. He did notice a pest-control person with mask and hand-sprayer get into a small truck.

He also noticed someone else. Later, as he was sitting on a shaded bench near the condominium, a blond lady made several passes, close by him, and appeared to be watching Leach's corner apartment. She looked thirtyish, could have been younger, Harry thought. Not really tanned, she wore glasses, and though not checking a watch, seemed to be on a schedule. He thought of Karri, but dismissed it. Wrong color hair? But if it were Karri, why wouldn't she be up on the deck, a drink in hand, doing meaningless things, relaxing. Still, she puzzled him. Then she was gone.

The following day he bought a white uniform, called the pest-control people and told them to have a man at 101 Waterway Drive at half past one. After exchanging greetings, things moved quickly. Harry realized the pest man wasn't the sharpest tool in the shed. Besides, he was called out to spray bugs, not question people's intentions. Harry explained who he was, Mr. Leach's brother and had seen the pest man the day before, tried to catch him, saw a roach, and if he had an extra sprayer and mask, he'd like to help. The pest man nodded in agreement. Forgetting his brother's card, he'd have to call an elderly neighbor—notes he had taken the day before. Harry handed the pest guy a hundred dollar bill, for his extra effort, and to let Harry do the talking. The neighbor came to the wide-corner balcony as the pest man gathered his equipment.

"Here yesterday," Harry yelled, pulling up the mask. "Missed Leach's. My mistake!"

She stared at Harry, at the other pest man, and at the lettered truck behind them.

"No one there?" she piped. "She was in a few minutes ago."

"Probably just being cautious," Harry choked.

"Here there, I'll come down. I'll knock for you," she said, smiling comfortably. A kindly lady.

Who was there, Harry wondered. Who was in a few minutes ago? Whoever it was, if she were gone, he would wait until she returned.

With masks on, sprayers in hand, they followed the lady. She knocked, no answer. They waited.

"I'll call Mr. Allen, the manager. Nope," she interrupted herself. "We'll take the inside elevator. Won't bother Mr. Allen for a key. More ways than one to skin a cat," she said, sprightly. Harry felt ten years younger.

She left them in the apartment, spraying. She called twice, monitoring their progress. He was sure she'd watch them leave. The apartment was beautifully appointed, Harry thought. An eight-foot glass panel etched with a sailfish dominated the living room. He thought of his office door. Everything was modern: glass, stainless, brushed aluminum, fogged mirrors. It was impersonal, corporate looking. The apartment was being used, however. At least someone had been there. Coffee grounds were on the counter, cigarettes in the ashtray, a door askew. Little things that didn't look like the Hinckley or the cottage on Beaver Island.

As the pest man walked out, the blond lady Harry had seen the day before walked in. Not turning her back to Harry, she pushed the door shut with a high heel. She removed her glasses, less business like and more elegant. She inhaled from a long cigarette, and watched as he dropped the mask and sprayer.

"Who are you?" she asked in the guttural voice of a smoker.

"Who are you?" Harry answered. There was no response. She held her ground.

"I asked who you were." She bore down, inhaling. She waited.

"Karri?"

Their eyes met, but she was staring beyond him, concentrating, as if seeking some distant recollection.

"Who are you? Yesterday I saw you on the bench, checking the place out. Who are you?" She asked.

Her presence intimidated Harry. Much as Laura had, he thought. He folded.

"I'm Harry Jones. I'm on a mission. To find Laura Nelson's daughter. Are you Karri?"

He had not been sure this was Karri. Was this the Karri in the photograph? A faint smile came to her face. Harry tried to figure it out. Not a conquering, triumphant smile. Not rolling the dice and hitting the seven, either. It was more of a smile of recollection.

"How difficult was it?" she asked. She turned toward the glass panel separating the living room from the outer balcony.

"Finding me," she finished, shaking her head, drawing on a dying cigarette.

"More time flying than figuring it out." Now being a detective and feeling a need to reestablish himself. He continued. "You're not exactly what I expected to find."

"What do you mean by that?"

"Glassy-eyed, emaciated, addicted, rolled up in the corner. Hell, I don't know."

She sighed, and then exhaled. She had not turned and faced Harry.

"I like him," she shrugged. "We meet halfway. That's it. Laura and Victor, Dad, have really gone overboard on this one. *Dad,*" she said turning to Harry, "has made too much of this."

She crossed the living room, moving closer to Harry. She propped herself on a tall counter stool, pulling an ashtray to herself. Harry sat down for the first time, in a hard steel chair, and watched as she lit another cigarette. She had beautiful athletic legs, and an independent air about her that seemed much older than twenty-eight. And under the control of Jack Leach? Laura, more probably Victor, *had* overreacted, Harry concluded. He would call Laura.

"I'll go back, tell Laura that I have found you, and settle up. You have a number where they can reach you?"

"I'll call them."

"Do you have a number?"

"I'll call them," she insisted.

"I need a number."

She looked at Harry.

"You know, you've got balls as big as watermelons. Pulling that shit about the pest control. Jesus," she shook her head, smiled, and Harry instantly grew from five-foot-ten to six-foot-four. Then she became serious.

"I want to ask you something."

"Yes." He said.

"Could I have a problem with Jack? Is there something I should know?"

Harry started, and then caught himself. Why would she be asking him about Jack? He was hired to find her, not investigate Jack Leach. Or was he overreacting? Maybe she figured he had stepped onto something during the search. Watch yourself, Harry, he thought. You're onto something big, don't ruin it. The time will come for confiding, for boasting, for reactions, but this isn't it. This isn't the right person, or the time, or the place. Yet, there should be a warning. As keen-minded as she seemed to Harry, a hint of caution wouldn't harm.

"You know what he does for a living?" stated Harry.

"A car dealer in Michigan."

"Ever been to his place?" Harry asked.

She hesitated and stared through him as she had done earlier when they met.

"His business?"

"Yes."

"Never."

"Been on the boat?" he asked.

"Saw it." she replied.

"Been to Beaver Island?"

"One time."

"The cedar-shake cottage, with the tower?"

She hesitated, crushed the cigarette and turned from him.

"What do you think?"

"I think," Harry caught himself.

"I'll tell you what I think," she interrupted, "I think we're both on track." She said no more, and he left with a phone number verified.

On the flight back to Detroit, there was a curiosity about Karri. It was like neither of them really belonged at that place at that time. Like both, on separate missions, just happened along at the same moment; both in their own way, seeking something more important. He couldn't put it together, but he had more important things to do, and he left it at that.

A driver! Like God had answered their call, the loud-mouthed sales-manager bellowed to his salesman. They were looking at Harry as they laughed. There was something unpleasant about being back in a dealership, Harry thought. He had butterflies in his stomach. It was like going back to school years after you'd graduated.

"The last guy quit cause he got twenty bucks for a five-hour trade. Cheap bastard didn't remember all the two-hour runs. The fucker! The thankless cocksucker should've been happy. With all the fucking lay-offs, the fuckin' bastard."

With that, Harry became a driver for Jack Leach Chrysler.

He quickly found that either the help didn't know Jack Leach very well or were awfully closemouthed. Little was said to or about him. The place seemed to run in spite of him. The anticipated first hand shake, or rather nod, proved anticlimatic. Jack Leach neither recognized Harry's name nor his face. The driving started immediately. Harry was surprised, considering how few cars they sold.

It was on the third trade that he first recognized something strange. He and a shop helper drove to another dealership to buy a car outright. He liked the helper because he was the only one with whom Harry could confide, probably having something to do with their status. When they got to the other dealership, they found the car to be identical to one already on the Leach lot. The helper was positive because he had cleaned the other car—same color, same packages, same everything. Harry called back to the dealership.

"The boss wants it. Just get the car."

When they returned, the sales-manager, obviously irritated, took Harry aside. "This happens. I don't know why. Just get the fuckin' cars, okay?"

The manager, bigger and younger than Harry, stuck his finger into Harry's chest. "Okay. Do you read me?"

"No fucking problem," Harry returned, to the surprise of both.

Later he checked the cars. They were identical. Both sat on the lot unsold. He couldn't put his finger on it. He'd been in the car business long enough to know dealers didn't stock cars just to stock cars. The floor plan interest to dealers was just too great. It was one of the biggest expenses at a car dealership. Mega-dealers duplicated models because of their turnover, but Leach Chrysler wasn't exactly a mega-dealer.

Two days later he was called for a similar trade, another direct buy. This time it was a club-cab pickup. It was in

Indiana, a six-hour trip. Harry figured he'd be in good favor with the sales-manager after this one. He sat glumly in the car as the mechanic's helper drove. He felt depressed. He wasn't making headway like he thought. He wasn't infiltrating the place at all. He wished he lived closer, because he knew it was there, somewhere. He just had to find it. He doubted if the sales-manager was a part of this; he didn't seem smart enough to Harry, nor did anyone else he'd seen at the dealership. Definitely not the "front end" people.

The mechanic's helper also was unimpressed with "the front end people," as he called the salesmen and sales-manager. To him, the "back end" guys, the mechanics, were the cream. He thought the owner was one of them. Harry noticed that there didn't seem to be any "look out for the boss" attitude with the sales force. In fact, there was no air about him that even slightly hinted that he was even a part of the sales department. Harry's experience had taught him that a dealer's top priority was always the sales department... service, parts, they were well down the list of importance. Did he know Jack Leach? Sure he did; a real family man—three kids, little leagues, on city boards, past president of the Chamber of Commerce.

"A down-home, wifey, churchie kinda guy," Harry added.

"Yeah. You know 'em too?"

The mechanic's helper continued. "Always around the dealership. You know, when he's around. Hands-on man."

That remark surprised Harry, because no one else seemed to be slightly aware of Jack Leach's presence. "Doing what?" he asked his companion.

"Just in the back a lot, you know. Hands-on kinda boss. Checkin' service jobs. Checkin' be-backs. You know, what comes back when it ain't fixed right. You know, always in and out. Preps new cars, too. Not all of 'em, you know."

"Prepping new cars?" Harry laughed. "Getting them ready for delivery?"

"Yeah, I ain't kiddin'. You know, not all of 'em. Some of 'em."

"New cars for delivery?" Harry said it slowly, looking straight ahead. "The dealer? The owner of the dealership?"

"Sure, you know, comes in at night. Not to get in us mechanics' way. Gets 'em ready for delivery. Even stock units. I really admire 'em for that, you know, being the owner and everything."

The talking exhausted Harry's friend, whose mind was suddenly empty, and he stopped conversing. Harry sat up in the seat.

"Wait a minute. You mean the owner comes in at night, preps cars, cleans them. So the deadbeat salesmen don't have to lift a finger?"

"Right on. I admire 'em for it, you know. I wouldn't do it for the sleazebags. You know, 'less it was my job. Wait 'n see. He'll be in tonight. Always does the dealer trades. Loves them club cabs."

"Always the dealer trades," Harry repeated.

Attached to the check was a copy of the invoice for the truck they were purchasing. Harry studied the invoice. Nothing extraordinary except the point of origin was Tuluca, Mexico. The first thing to enter his mind was Mexico—cheap labor. The second thing was Mexico—drugs! Could there be a connection, he asked himself. The drive back from Indiana suddenly grew much shorter.

He jumped out of the truck and went up to the first salesman he could find, asking him if he'd been the lucky seller.

"No, it's not sold. But a great piece. I'll cut a hog in the ass with that one!"

A confident salesman, Harry thought. An asset to any dealership. He went to the car he had traded several days earlier. The point of origin on the window sticker read Tuluca, Mexico. He checked every dealer trade; they were all Neon's and club-cab pickups, and they were all manufactured in Tuluca.

He asked the same salesman, "Are Neons and club cabs the only vehicles Chrysler builds in Mexico?"

"The only spics there are chief."

Harry thought, "Those sons-of-a-bitches. They load them with drugs in Mexico, ship them north, and notify Leach where they'll be delivered. Because of his small allocation he can't get all of them himself, so he trades for those sent to other dealers. Or buys them outright. Anyway, he gets the cars with the drugs. And that is how the drugs end up on a plane on North Fox Island!"

With a feeling of pride and an exhilarated confidence about himself, Harry started for home. He made it as far as Lansing before turning back. One thing remained: Jack prepping cars at night, keeping out of the mechanics' way, accommodating salesmen. Shit, he thought. He laughed aloud. A hands-on kind of boss, an inspiring man, that Jack Leach, kind of guy you really wanted to admire.

He drove past Dewitt. Fifteen miles further north, in St. Johns, he sat in a coffee shop and planned. He'd wait until dark to confirm his suspicions.

Walking from across an alley and behind the dealership, in the shadows of the service department, he looked through a grease-smeared window. Jack Leach was in the far-corner stall, the prep stall, partially inside the truck Harry had driven from Indiana that day. He was meticulously working at something in the roof area. The glass was smeared on the inside so Harry quietly moved from the back of the dealership to the side service entrance. It was unlocked. For a second he hesitated, holding the turned handle. Prodding himself, he eased the door open. Why not? North Fox Island had done that for Harry. He was inside. If he were discovered, he'd lost his billfold and returned to check the truck. Simple—easier than the pest-control guy! The overhead heater clicked on, and Jack Leach, busy with the prep job, didn't notice the shadow in the darkened service area move within thirty feet of him. He had dropped the headliner on the truck. Taped to the inner portion were rows of plastic bags. Propped inside, between the split seats, were the mail pouches.

Confirmed, you son-of-a-bitch, thought Harry. He backed away in the general direction of the service door. Jack was engrossed in his work. Suddenly the furnace stopped with an abrupt whine—just as Harry's foot caught the loose end of a drop-cord, sending the wire-encased light bouncing across the floor. Jack whirled out of the truck, now sixty feet from Harry.

"Anyone here?" Harry yelled as loud as he could, staring directly at Jack in the darkness.

"You wait!" Jack Leach commanded. "Wait right there."

He shot through the confused, dimly lit rear of the building. His head hit the hanging lube gun, momentarily throwing his head back with a loud, "Jesus."

"Mr. Leach?"

"What in hell are you doing here?"

"Lost my billfold," Harry said softly, speaking each word as distinctively as possible.

"Thought maybe I had left it in the truck I picked up today. Hoped it would be outside—unlocked. The service door was open and."

"I'm prepping it," Jack interrupted. "I didn't see your billfold, but I'll look. You wait right there." He pointed to a spot on the floor.

"No, sir, not here," Leach shouted from sixty feet.

"What about the car Harold drove you down in?" Leach added as he approached Harry.

"The loaner van, that's an idea, Mr. Leach."

Jack Leach grabbed the key from the service desk and escorted Harry outside, locking the service door behind him. The service van was unlocked. After a check, Mr. Leach gave Harry his condolences and asked if he needed a "ten spot" to get home.

"No, Mr. Leach, I've the twenty from the trade. I'll call tomorrow. See if it shows up. Thanks for your time, Mr. Leach." He left it hanging.

"No problem, uh-er," he'd forgotten Harry's name. Prepping the truck was Jack Leach's first big concern.

Going home that night, Harry drove faster them he'd ever driven in his life. His euphoria overwhelmed him. His stomach cramped, his legs shook, he alternated between a hot and cold sweat. He had never been so excited.

"Christ, I'm a kid! I'm a sixty-year-old, retired kid," he announced profoundly to himself. But he could not sleep that night.

Harry could always sleep. He prided himself on the fact. He considered it an asset. But tonight Laura kept him awake. Thinking of nothing but calling her; her composure, the tone of her voice, the heightened anxiety as the story unfolded. Finding Karri would be incidental. It *was* the Jack Leach story now.

Harry wanted this to happen in his office. At his pace. He wanted to see her totally engrossed as he wove the incidents together. He wanted to see her amazed at his skill. She was an I-me person, he knew, but now she would listen to him intently, spellbound by the events.

He saw himself asking for her advice, then watching her composure fade. Harry needed that, because it was as an important a part of this whole affair as contacting the Drug Enforcement Agency and bringing Jack Leach down. It would not be an overkill, but it would be more than business as usual.

She had never left a call on his answering machine before; now there were four calls, each with a different return number, each instructing him not to use his own phone and each asking him to clear the tape on his answering machine. No sign of anxiety, just the same demanding monotone. He called her at the last number from a pay phone. Laura answered, asked for his number, and told him to wait for a return call. Five minutes later, she was calling from a car phone.

"Harry, I want you to meet me. In three days. In the Catskills. Write this down, Lew Beach, New York, Beaverkill Inn. Ever been there?" she asked, lightly.

"No, but—."

"Knew you hadn't. It's two and a half hours from New York. Your ticket's at Metro. Flight two nineteen. A rental car will be waiting."

"But—."

"No, no, no, Harry. No buts—don't say anything, please. I need to see you now!"

"Why the Catskills?" he shot back before she could hang up on him. There was a pause.

"Because it's a wonderful place for fly-fishing. I called for you. You were either fly-fishing, or learning. I didn't get it straight. But," she said lightly, "if you want to learn fly-fishing, this is the place. And I am going to be your instructor." she added. "Seriously, Harry. I want to speak with you... now."

An old headache started to return. What had happened to the other scenario, he asked himself. The old "at my pace" scenario, with Harry Jones in control?

The inn was a nineteenth century anglers' lodge. His room had been reserved. He thought the posted price a little steep considering the shared bath. As he returned from the shower, the phone was ringing. It was Laura.

"Come down when you're ready. I'm in front of this wonderful fireplace, did you have a good flight?"

"If there is such a thing."

Laura's voice had a different tone—a light, airier quality to it. At first he thought it could be someone else.

She was sipping a Manhattan as he sat down across from her. Between them was a low table made of birch. Encased under a glassed top were dried moths and butterflies, surrounded by river moss. A natural look filled the room: fly rods with reels, landing nets, wicker creels. There were fishing vests with forceps and flies, worn waders with suspenders. A comfortable place for a not-too-comfortable Harry Jones.

"Have a drink, Harry. It looks like you could use one."

He ordered a schnapps with ice.

"Your first?" he asked.

"No, second. Actually I'm feeling it a little," Laura said, crossing her legs. "It's been a long day for me, too." She squinted, then laughed. "Here, I'm already sharing secrets." It was the first time he had heard her laugh.

The drink settled in well, and Harry ordered a second.

"I worry for Karri, being with Leach. I should have called you when I first got back from Naples. But things happened."

There was a pause, then Laura said, "I know. She called. Thanks very much. Here's to Karri," Laura tipped her glass toward Harry with sarcasm. She lit a cigarette, tilting her head upward, away, and then blew the smoke above him, not taking her eyes from him. She did not speak, and there was another uneasy pause.

Harry looked at her and said, "And I found more. A lot more."

"Jack Leach?"

"Yes. Jack Leach."

Leaning forward, close to her, he began the story of events, moving from Leach, to Beaver Island, to Fox Island, to Naples, and to the dealership. Listening intently, she often looked beyond him into the fire, occasionally glancing back, meeting the eyes that never left her. She refolded her legs, sometimes massaging them. On her third cigarette and well into the business of drugs, she raised a hand as if to stop.

"Can we have dinner, Harry?"

He followed her in silence into the dining room, dimmed now for the evening setting. There were several parties of four and six, a few couples, mostly subdued, and only a light laughter among them. Not exactly the Shamrock at happy hour, Harry thought.

They sat across from each other at a small table. He ordered drinks. With arms crossed on the table, Harry continued his story. As he spoke he watched her. Sometimes Laura seemed almost in a trance, boring into his chin and lips with her gaze. Then glancing up into his eyes, never disbelieving, transfixed with his details about North Fox Island.

They ordered soup, an Italian leek. He talked through the salad, the panned trout, the glasses of Riesling, and into a rather skimpy slice of plain cheesecake. When they reached after dinner coffee and the correlation between Neon's, club cab pickups, and Tuloca, Mexico, Laura leaned well back in her chair, sighed, lifted both arms high and behind her, and pushed her fingers through her hair, leaving vulnerable both her lovely figure and her overwhelming thoughts. He had not seen her so affected before. He felt pleased with himself, not in a chauvinistic way, only because Laura had reacted just as Harry had expected. Just as he had hoped.

"I should act now, shouldn't I, Laura? I mean with the drug enforcement people."

He was asking for an answer to a question with a foregone conclusion that he didn't get, and that had something to do with why he was in the Catskill Mountains with her that night.

In a very calm, yet calculated voice, she said, "I don't want you to do anything, Harry."

"What?" Harry gasped.

"I want you to stop now."

"Stop? Now! What...?"

"Forget everything you've told me and just end it. Could you do that?"

This was now her new tone—not demanding, not abrupt, just asking in an almost imploring way.

"How the hell can I do that? Why...?"

She interrupted by putting her hand on his arm.

"Is there any way I could tell you it's going to be handled? Any way I can confide without you asking? Assuring that it's going to happen—soon. Harry, without going into it further right now, can we end it here?"

Harry leaned forward into her face. "How can you? What's happening?" he whispered. "I come out here, tell you a story no one in this world knows about, except me, and you somehow know enough about the whole thing to ask me out of it. Is it Karri? Is she threatened? Has Leach somehow found out about me and threatening? Is he after all of us—me, you, your stepdaughter? How big is this whole thing? I mean with you, Laura?" His gaze was stern, and he studied her closely. "I mean with you. You've never met him right? That is what you said, correct?"

"I have never met Jack Leach. I told you that, and it's the truth. I just need you to take yourself out of this and let it go."

Harry's head throbbed. Through the confusion, he knew Laura had answers.

"I've got to think, Laura. We'll tackle this in the morning."

He took his after dinner drink with him to his room. After showering, Harry looked at himself in the full-length mirror. He was as tall as he needed to be, and pleased he wasn't five-foot-six, but not feeling a need to be six-foot-two. His hair was gray, full, and easy to keep trimmed with the same "Princeton" style of forty years earlier. He carried no extra weight and, he mused, if he had cared, he could have been athletic; a golfer, approaching a good lie, walking briskly, confident of a pin-high second shot, as the commentators say. If he had cared. And then there's the people you have to play with in that game. He could at least have been well groomed, he thought. Seemed less of a bore. He had the physique for stylish dress, but in that he was also a creature of habit. He recalled his secretary once comparing him to a TV newsman, not being bigger than the news itself, but offering an air of credibility to it. Harry knew, without working at it, he had that credibility thing, partly because of his thirty-five years of experience, but mostly because along with the credibility came a certain indifference to consequence. That trait, more than anything else, had secured for him a working career of mediocrity. He knew it, and he accepted it. Now that career almost seemed like a different world to him.

He was standing in his towel, glass in hand, staring through the window into blackness, when there was a slight knock, a turned key, and Laura confronted him. She shut the door behind her and faced Harry. She had left her high heels and dress and was standing in slacks and a blouse. She unbuttoned her blouse and removed it, exposing her large, firm, low-slung breasts. She stepped out of her slacks and said quietly, "I'm naked, Harry. I want you to take me to bed."

Nerves, a fragile commodity, were something Harry held at a premium, and Harry was unnerved. Laura, however, in her own way, did a remarkable job of coaxing the very best out of Harry, and Harry, in return, felt quite good about himself.

The first impression Harry had was how physically strong she was; the second was how she handled the mechanics of her lovemaking, almost as if it were an obligation, a debt owed, a contract fulfilled.

Alice streaked through Harry's brain, and what he once playfully called one only manship was now gone in the most confusing way.

When Laura left she whispered in his ear, "Remember, Harry, fly-fishing tomorrow."

Lying in bed, he thought about her insistence that he let it go. He did not ask himself to let it go, nor did he understand her reasoning. Sleep caught up with him before the answer could be found. During the night he awoke wondering who Laura Nelson really was. What entered his mind was some vague relationship between Jack Leach, Laura Nelson, and her stepdaughter, Karri.

Earlier that evening, Harry and Laura had left the dining room together for their separate second-floor rooms, and she had parted with, "See ya, Harry." He had caught himself—his mind was elsewhere—and nodded as he passed her in the hallway. "Yes, see you in the morning, Laura."

When Laura returned to her room, she called for a drink—a perfect Manhattan, the drink she had started with that evening. She kicked off her heels, dropped into a large chair with an ottoman, stretched her legs, lit a cigarette, and exhaled with an audible sigh. Her mind was void of objectivity; an old paranoia was trying to return. Laura sat facing an inner-mirrored wall. The mirror painted a window with open Venetian blinds and a faded light somewhere in the darkened out-of-doors, and the now-and-again glow of a cigarette that gave a grotesque half view of a tilted head. She quickly turned to the floor lamp beside her. The shade was made of pearlized shells that were dulled by years of cigarette smoke.

The shade and the small, sparse room, although quaint in the fishing lodge, reminded her of something she could not forget and that her nightmares always forced her to remember. A young agent with a seasoned veteran. A young trainee scared. A senior agent with no fear, no feeling. A bad situation that could have became worse; only, he saved her life. She had fired her weapon, in self defense, but it was he who had saved her. Later, she knew she should not have drank with him, a celebration, a guy thing. He was callous; she was vulnerable. The nightmare always returned exactly the same, never modifying, never easing the truth, never helping her when she awoke and cried out. It was always exactly the same ordeal: he, forcing himself, she relinquishing. And finally, as he laughed, and later as he laughed with others, flipping her exhausted, incoherent body over, like a pancake, to be sodomized. It burned in her because it would never, ever let her go. Even the sudden demise of her nemesis would not help her.

The light from the shade rescued her from the mirror. She returned to the evening with Harry, trying to retrace it from the beginning to where it now stood. She rose and turned toward the window and confronted it: an outside lamp defined a canopied entrance, an oval driveway, and the trout ponds beyond. It annoyed her; it distracted from her thought process. It tried to confuse her. She turned to the phone, dismissed it, and ordered another drink.

The drink came, and, without a word, she initialed the card, slammed the door, and returned to the chair. This time she sat erect, her legs pulled upwards toward her. Angrily, she beaded into the mirror, as if sighting down the muzzle end of a gun. She was mad. She was mad at the drink, mad at her cigarette, mad at herself. The whole thing had gotten away from her, and she wondered where it was moving and what she was going to do. She would remain calm. She was angry with Harry Jones, if for no other reason than he was Harry Jones. But he had unwittingly tilted the scale. What were her options? She needed the control. She always needed that. Deliberately, she exchanged her dress for a pair of slacks. She removed her bra. She didn't need the assurance of looking at herself and ignored the mirror. She slowly buttoned her blouse and arranged it as she finished the perfect Manhattan and closed the door—and the mirror—behind her.

T he phone rang at seven. Wake up call. He hadn't asked for a wake up call. The phone rang again. It was Laura.

"I'll be waiting for you at breakfast. Ten minutes?"

"Make it fifteen," he said, with a push for self-respect.

She wore a long-sleeved, khaki blouse tucked into tight khaki trousers and smiled at him as they ate.

"I've got waders, rods, and reels, blankets, a lunch, wine. You name it."

"What do we do with the fish?" Harry asked.

"We're not catching any fish."

"What?"

"No…. We're not going fishing Harry. I'm going to show you how to fly-fish."

In four hours, on the Beaverkill River, the birthplace of dry fly-fishing in America, Harry was fly-casting.

"Remember," she yelled at Harry, "this may be the only sport in the world where you use the same amount of power in the back motion as you do in the forward motion. Get it?"

A four-count between ten and one o'clock. An arm action, no wrist, a subtle snap of the line so the fly and leader touched down in front of him in the water before the trailing line dropped behind them. Laura sat amused.

"You're casting only the line, Harry. Not like a casting or spinning outfit. The only weight is in the line—not the bait." Laura said, again screaming over the sound of the water.

It was straight casting, but he did it surprisingly well. She watched him and in a few moments realized that he was alone, innocently unaware, away from her, working the rod and line, miles from the decision that was inevitable. She knew it was coming, and she did not feel good about it. No fear, she just didn't feel good about it.

They sat cross-legged on the blanket, facing the other, laughing, Harry rejecting any thought of a compliment about his newfound skill. They drank the bottle of wine. He once caught a glimpse of sorrow when she looked away, and he called her on it. She twisted her shoulders, shrugging it off.

"Just a thought, pal." She hadn't used that expression before.

"A penny for it."

"It isn't worth it, Harry."

There was a pause.

"Harry—?" She stopped, left it at that. Then he knew she was changing the subject and the tone.

"Don't get too excited with your casting," she instructed him.

"It's not the presentation, those seventy-foot casts are movie crap. The fish you catch will be fifteen or twenty feet in front of you."

"Don't be too practical about this," he said.

"But the end result, Harry, is catching the fish, and remember, ninety percent of that is using the right bait."

"What about a perfect cast—in just the right spot. There's a reward in that."

"No, the reward is in catching the fish."

There was a touch of sarcasm in her voice. It went unrewarded. He shook his head.

"No compromise. Don't you ever compromise?"

Harry looked at Laura, smiled, and got a smug look in response.

"Last night, Harry," she said blankly, pulling on a cigarette. "Have you done that often…? I mean...."

"Never," he responded, emphatically.

She looked up at him and cried, "I knew you'd say that, Harry. Just like that, *never*," emphasizing the word.

"You are quite a man, Harry. Really, you're quite a guy."

After they returned to the inn, and he had told her he had to go through with it, and she pleaded only once, then left, it ran through Harry's mind. The compliment. The only compliment he ever really remembered: "You're quite a man, Harry. Quite a guy."

A week later and three days before his appointment with the Drug Enforcement Administration people, Harry

received a call from Laura. She sounded her old self—
resolved. Victor insisted on an accounting, so that he could
"square things" with Harry. He was insistent on being more
than fair. She had an idea. They would meet in Charlevoix,
at noon of the following day, at the ferry dock. They would
try his kind of fishing! He didn't consider resisting.

She had rented a twenty-five-foot inboard-outboard.

"Show me North Fox, Harry."

"It's a long way out."

"What's a long way?"

"Twenty-five miles."

"I don't care. The lake's smooth, only a slight fog."

They motored under the drawbridge, through the channel, out into the open water of Lake Michigan. Spray flying,
the boat pounded in the small chop. The engine and waves
were so loud that Laura hardly spoke. In an hour they were
midway between North and South Fox islands, miles from
either shore. Laura slowed the boat.

Laura turned to Harry. "There is no power, Harry. Like a
sheared pin. Would you check the prop with me?"

He moved to the rear, grabbing a side rail as the boat
lurched. He was in front of her, and, as he leaned over the
stern, she pushed.

Some say that hypothermia is a good way to go. Of
course, nobody who ever went that way could confirm it,
but Harry guessed that it must have been from someone's
near-death experience. He yelled for her to help as the boat
motored away in the fog. It was almost a humorous cry. But
the humor and the panic were both killed by the cold. At
first he thought she was only disoriented, that the fog
would clear and she would return. Then he could hear the
drumming of the engine becoming more distant. In forty-
degree water you first lose control of your feet, then your
arms. Finally your senses become dulled, and a calm comes
over you.

Harry swam hard for several minutes. The experts say that's bad; it causes body heat to leave the core faster. And it exhausted him. He remained motionless for several seconds. His feet were numb and he could no longer use his arms. He thought the drumming had been replaced with a cur-jung, cur-jung, but sounds were now confused, and there was no vibration to feel in the still water, only that the water now seemed to be warming. His senses were calming and wearisome, and he could not see land anymore. He could not see Alice Henrietta or her stained glass; he could only hear her quiet laughter. He did see Jack Leach and his packets of drugs, then he too was gone. He thought of a Gordon Lightfoot song now that time seemed irrelevant. He got a glimpse of Laura, and she stayed with him longer—stern, demanding, always that authority about her, even when she pleaded, needing his help. Even when she cried, there was never a tear. Yet she needed him. She did need him, didn't she? Then she was above him, naked and alone, making love. Finally she was laughing and crying again, hugging him, and saying, "You are quite a man, Harry, really...." He smiled and ceased shaking. Then he was gone.

An Indian fisherman, as it was reported in the news, working his nets between North and South Fox, found a partially-collapsed inflatable. A rod and reel was still in the boat; an electric motor was still attached. The police found Harry Jones' identification in a fishing box tied to an oar lock. But they didn't find Harry Jones.

Five months later, at eight-thirty in the morning, the phones were ringing on every line in every office at Chrysler Corporation headquarters in Auburn Hills. They were also ringing at Chrysler's Detroit zone office in Troy. Facts were needed in Auburn Hills; the press would demand a statement. Auburn Hills, ready as usual to distance themselves from any dealer's personal problems, wanted something on Jack Leach—anything.

The headlines told the rest. Greatest Drug Bust-Ever! At one end a Chrysler Corporation dealer, on the other end, members of Mexico's political elite and New York City's social and economic powerhouses. A Washington connection; details to follow. So heavy with influence some even speculated about the collapse of NAFTA. Two days of national news stories and commentary.

Then an even bigger story. The two federal narcotic people responsible for the bust were female agents. And not just female agents. When their pictures first appeared, they were not believable. Camille Thurston and Victoria Nelson were much too good looking. The public's perception of the narcotics business was too vile for these movie-like people. One appeared almost childlike, an exuberant blond, athletic, wide-eyed, smiling. The other, dark hair, more statuesque, with a model-like reluctance about her. Stories and substories appeared everywhere. Their childhoods—one from the rural Midwest, the other from New York. Their meeting as college roommates, and their bonding with youthful idealism and the difference they would make. How it all came together as junior agents in the Drug Enforcement Agency.

Then it became more unbelievable. Coverage moved from the glamorous to their life as agents. There had been a feminist movement within the department. It had not been brought to the public's attention. These two were the leaders. They had been working in an agency, almost in spite of it, so wrought with dissension that it was near collapse. They had been outspoken about the need for change. They had refused to leave the department because of overt sexism, as some had, nor would they accept it as most had who remained. They had fought it with tenacity, and now they had won on the highest level, that of achievement. The media reported that the end of sexism in the federal bureaucracy had finally been achieved. With this crushing blow to international drug trade, delivered by two female agents, machismo forever ceased to exist in the federal government. That was the way the media interpreted it, that was the way the press wrote it, and that was the way the public accepted it.

Within days these two women appeared on the nation's most watched mid-evening talk show. People saw the photographs, read all the stories, heard every imaginable commentary, but nothing stirred their interest as much as a person-to-person interview on television.

As the host began his interview, a retired detective sat at a desk in a small study in a wintered up village in northern Michigan and he turned to the TV and watched with interest.

The female agents sat across from their host; one seemed promiscuously upbeat, the other cautiously serene. Sitting in front of the TV, he was not quite sure. Cami, as she was called, didn't look tough enough. She should have been skiing in Colorado, or surfing in Malibu, on a Miller Lite ad, hoisting a beer—fresh, exuberant, erotic. There should have been battle scars, but they weren't evident. He couldn't picture Victoria haunting drug houses, working with unshaven, unkempt narc agents. He couldn't imagine her being one of them. He could not imagine her being able to comprehend the total deprivation of the drug dealer's world or the vulgarity of the users. But then he knew that is what made these people something special, why they were on national television, being interviewed, and he was sitting in his lazyboy at home. Why they are they, and you are you, he thought.

The host asked Cami how she was reacting to all the coverage. She had loved it at first. But now she wanted to get back to work. What about all this movie stuff, writing a book? Definitely no book, and the movie stuff was somebody's imagination gone wild. Would she stay with the agency? No, probably not. She glanced at Victoria, who had been watching her throughout the interview. She would enjoy a slower pace, teaching perhaps. At a small college—law. Yes, the host knew she had a law degree. George Washington University, wasn't it? She didn't say it, but Cami had already accepted a professorship in South Dakota, in the law school of a small university.

The host was mesmerized by Victoria. He was asking the questions to Cami, but he was intent on her associate. Victoria was unaware of it. It didn't make her nervous. He then turned to Victoria, asked specifically about the case, the drug bust. She spoke calmly, in generalities. He asked how they discovered the method by which the drugs were brought into the country, in the headliners of the vehicles. She looked to Cami, then leaned forward, toward her host. She apologized for inadvertently calling him Harry instead of Larry. He made a small thing out of it, saying he wished he were Harry, whoever Harry was, and she laughed, touching his outstretched arm. She explained how the exact modus operandi could not be disclosed. For the protection of other agents in the field. What about a phantom agent? The *Times* had created the story. The job was so big! By *no* means sounding macho, he blurted, arousing a good laugh by all three, and the back stage people, but how could just the two, in the field alone, accomplish this whole thing? He was truly amazed, he said. And he was....

"No phantom agent, Larry. A lot of help from a number of people. But no phantom agent."

The lightness of the conversation changed the viewers' perception immediately. Victoria's laugh and smile and gestures now made her one of the three. Her aloofness was gone, and she was part of them. The viewers had wanted to like her. Yes, she was going to stay with the agency. It had been her life and would continue to be; there was so much more in this war on drugs. Did she now feel a new status for women in these agencies? Yes, she did, and yes, there had been habitual harassment, sexism, it was well documented. But that was behind her now. It was behind the agency.

Someday, could she run an agency like the D.E.A.? It wasn't beyond her wildest dreams, she replied. Victoria did not mention that she already knew within weeks she would be promoted to an assistant deputy administrator.

The host felt he had a good show. He knew he had the ratings. After a short summation, the interview ended. The host turned directly to several million viewers, stating this was a truly memorable experience for him as the host, allowing him a lasting belief that these were our country's finest, in their finest moments, models to make every American proud. He shook their hands and winked at Victoria. As they left, Victoria put her arm over Cami's shoulder. No one, the host, the millions watching, maybe not even the two of them, realized the depths of the passion that each had for the other.

The retired detective stirred the embers of his dying fire. He turned off the TV and went to bed.

Months passed, spring came to Michigan, and the arts and crafts people were busy preparing for the summer shows. There was a knock on Alice Henrietta's door and a tall, dark-haired lady in slacks and sweater stood waiting. She wore sunglasses, a cap pulled well down on her forehead.

Alice introduced herself. The lady was passing through, had known Harry, had remembered him speaking of Alice Henrietta and her work.

"You are busy. But could I see your work?" the lady asked.

Alice was overjoyed with the compliment, as always, and invited her into the workshop to see the year's project.

Her house was full of small papier-mache' boxes, smaller than hat boxes. They were of all shapes—heart, square, octagon, strange shapes, like individual candy boxes, but larger.

Alice explained to the stranger how she and the ladies prepared their work. The plain boxes were covered and trimmed, using old Christmas paper, cuts of Victorian scenes, the Impressionists, Currier and Ives prints, a collage of cows and cats—everything. The art of decoupage. The images were adhered with a paste called "mod podge," which, when dry, came clear with a hard finish. Then, with acrylics and stencil paints, the ladies painted flowers and trees, butterflies, personal things. Finally, to take on a patina, stain was used. Alice nudged the younger lady's arm, she was disclosing a secret. When the boxes dried, a polyurethane was painted on to preserve them. Oh, and they were signed. All the ladies now signed their own work. Alice was indeed proud of the boxes. The stranger moved slowly among the rooms of boxes, admiring them all. Alice presented her with a box as a gift.

But she had to leave; time had flown, but she so enjoyed meeting Alice. Alice thought she should make an inquiry, after consuming the lady with herself and her work.

"You once worked with Harry?"

"Yes."

"One of his prodigies?" She laughed. "So many girls went on to bigger dealerships as office managers. You live near here?"

"No, not in Michigan."

A short pause and Alice added, "You know Harry died."

"Yes, I'm sorry."

Victoria turned to Alice. "Don't think I'm being rude, but," she hesitated, "they never recovered Harry's body, did they?"

"No, that far north, on the Great Lakes, we've been told the lakes don't often give up their dead."

"Speaking of Harry," Alice continued, "I had an interesting guest months ago now. An Indian from Beaver Island who knew Harry. It was so strange. He spoke like he'd known Harry for ages."

"Were you suspicious?"

"At first. But then he talked of things—about Harry's job, about my crafts, about Harry's past. I realized he really knew Harry. It was almost mystic, as though he was trying to discover something in me that he could relate to Harry and himself."

"Some people grieve that way," Victoria said.

"Oh, I don't think he was grieving. Just relating I think."

"What was his name?" she asked.

"John Peltier. He was a commercial fisherman. He was the one that found the boat Harry was using."

The lady turned to Alice Henrietta, smiled, and let her continue. "They had to know each other, but it could only have been for a short time—a few weeks. Harry had never been on Beaver Island in his life until a few weeks before he drowned. The Indian seemed honest though. A caring person. It was just a surprise. A tall, handsome Indian with a pony tail, coming to the house, talking about Harry," Alice laughed. "The things you find out about someone you think you know so well."

"I've experienced that myself," the lady returned, concentrating on Alice Henrietta's remarks.

Another lady, overhearing the conversation, added, "Alice and the girls recently erected a memorial at Oak Hill Cemetery. It's beautiful."

It was still new, and Alice in her excitement offered to take the visitor to see it.

"Thank you, Alice. But another time, I'll see it. I'm running awfully late. I adore your work. I'll find a very special place for this," she said, gesturing with her gift.

They shook hands and waved goodbyes. She would go to the cemetery, but she wanted to go alone. She had sought a finality to this, but somehow she knew she would not find it.

The cemetery keeper pointed the direction to the memorial and she found it easily. It was a large stone of black granite. The letters were cut in gray and were simply: "In Memory of Harry Jones" with the dates of his life. Above the lettering was a small oval piece of leaded glass, embossed on the black granite. She stepped forward. It had two painted words, and it was signed "A.H." She smiled and put her gloved hand to her lips, and then her composure was gone, and she cried, and, for an instant, she was confused by her thoughts. Were they for Harry Jones, or were they for Cami Thurston? Or were they just for Victoria Nelson?

She stepped back, still crying. For several moments she gazed at the stone. Then she walked to her car and drove away.

The wind blew through the Norway pines that surrounded the cemetery, an eerie voice not unlike the sound of surf pounding a faraway shore. It was forewarning a summer storm that had already passed over Beaver Island, two hundred and fifty miles to the northwest.

Alone at a corner table—his table—in the Shamrock, John Peltier, the fisherman, was finishing his third and last beer and listening intently to a table of tourists telling what little they knew of certain myths of the Great Lakes, one stating as if fact that the upper lakes never gave up their dead. They all agreed they had heard the story. The mirror behind the bar reflected a private grin on John's face when he rose to leave.

Approaching their table none mistook the fact that he was an Indian. Looking down at them he said, "So the myth has it the Big Lake never gives up her dead. That is interesting, but...," he mocked, raising a finger, "I think it is not always so. No, believe me, it is not always true."

His eyes sparkled as he shuffled out of the door into the darkness and toward his cabin in the woods. The tourists had no idea what the Indian was talking about. John didn't talk much, and some thought a newfound liveliness about him was due to the light winter, the lack of solid ice that usually closed the harbor, and thus his ability to fish most of the past winter. He had let the transient go, and he and his Indian helper fished alone.

Sometimes a third man was seen on the boat, a bearded man in an oversized mackinaw with a stocking cap well down on his forehead. John never talked about the man and the man had never been seen in the Shamrock. When asked, John's mother only shrugged her shoulders, and said it was just an old friend John had taken in... just to help the old man out.

PART TWO

"Each of us needs to be a hero to someone. It is in all of us."

That is how the conversation started one morning at the Early Bird, the only morning cafe open during the winter months in Leland, Michigan. Around the big table, over coffee, a half dozen of the village's residents met six days a week. One of the men, a retired professor, got into the conversation. He said, "You know, we all want to be someone's hero. There is a need for men—like there's a need in women to have children."

"Age have anything to do with it?"

"Nothing, whatever." He paused, then added, "Maybe the need seems greater—as years become more defining."

"It's not all that easy," someone interrupted.

"For some it is... being our own hero works quite well. That is easy, our egos can handle that for us."

"But some resist this self fulfillment."

"You're right. And that's making it work the right way."

One of those sitting at the table was Tom Morgan. He was retired, a widower, and, unknown to everyone in the

Early Bird that morning; he wasn't feeling particularly good about himself. The talk about heroes caught his attention. He had been a policeman in Leland for thirty-two years. When he retired he was the detective. He had two grown sons; both were educated and successful, each with a loving wife and each with young children. They both lived in other states, hundreds of miles from Leland. For one thing, Tom now felt a void his earlier life had not produced. He tried to understand, with little success, the parental love he received from his sons. He felt there wasn't any particular respect about it. It surprised him that even his grandchildren weren't in the slightest awe of either him or his profession. He sometimes felt he thought about it too much and, more often than not, concluded it was foolish thinking. Thinking about the conversation that morning and about his sons and their wives and his grandchildren, about love and respect, he thought he was being a little reactionary, probably a little foolish. Still, all and all, Tom wanted to be their hero.

There was an uneasiness about Tom that others had noticed. Some of his friends thought he retired too early, but they knew there were money problems in Leland and that his position was never filled. Some thought he was still grieving over his wife's death. It had been difficult; theirs was a single life for forty-one years. Most, however, liked Tom for what he was, a quiet man in a quiet town, involved in community projects, at church every Thursday night and Sunday morning. And he helped at the marina during the busy months of July and August.

Walking home from the cafe to his small house on Front Street, past the closed shops, Tom wondered what it would be like to live some place that was open all year. Leelanau County was one of the smallest countys in Michigan, and, if you looked at it on the map, it was the "little finger" of Michigan's geographic mitten. Over one hundred miles of shoreline. Leland, with a population of five hundred, was the county seat. During the four months of the "season" it was crowded with summer residents, vacationers, and boat people. Then everything was closed. The boats were stored for the winter; the vacationers went back to their jobs; and the summer people closed up their cottages and flew to winter homes in Florida and Arizona.

Tom Morgan's house overlooked Lake Michigan. It was a small, cedar-shake Cape Cod that was twenty years old when he and his wife, Anne, purchased it in 1955. Close on each side were larger, boarded up summer homes. Now in mid-winter, covered with snow and surrounded with six-foot high drifts, the house was isolated even from Leland. Inside, the house seemed even smaller. On the main floor an entrance, small kitchen, living room and a small study faced the lake through a wide, now snow-blown porch. A large, well used open fireplace dominated the living room. Bookshelves covered most of the two open walls, as well as the walls in the study. A small fireplace, backed to the larger one in the living room, made the study appear crowded. Tom's books were in this room. Detective books. Some mysteries, books on fishing, shipwrecks on the Great Lakes, Ernest Hemingway, but mostly detective novels. Agatha Christie and Dorothy Sayers were his favorites. *Murder at the Vicarage* was still his favorite, *Dead Man's Folly* ran a close second. Most of Tom Morgan's detective work was in these books. There had been only one murder in Leland in twenty-nine years. It involved an elderly lady poisoning an elderly man with arsenic over a very long period of time; the case had been handled by the county and state police. Two large, three-by-four foot nautical charts covered one wall of the study. One was Waugashance PT to Seul Choix PT., chart 14911, which included Beaver Island and its surrounding islands. The other was Platte Bay to Leland, chart 14912, which included the western shore of the Leelanau Peninsula, the

Manitou Islands, and the Fox Islands. The soundings were in feet, and Tom knew these charted areas well.

Tom added a log to the fire as he dropped the Detroit paper on the study desk. Later, sitting at his desk chair, he watched the ice roll out in the lake. So far it had not been a hard winter, and the lake was mush for only several hundred yards, then dark water. There were years when the lake froze solid, then it was all white. When that happened the wind drove the snow ashore into ten-foot drifts. He spent most of his time in the study. It had been Anne's favorite room. She loved the fire during the cold months. Now he burned the fire for her as much as for himself.

The phone rang. It was detective Walter Shipman, a close friend from the Charlevoix County Sheriff's Department.

"Rogue! How are you doing?" Walter asked.

For all those years as a policeman, Tom Morgan had been the antithesis of a rogue cop. So the nickname stuck.

"As per usual. Yourself?"

"Busy. Doing a lot with the schools. I'm getting to be a real expert on drugs."

"You don't have a big problem up there?"

"Not really. Don't want one either. More trouble during the summer. Down-staters, the "fudgies," when they leave they seem to take most of it back with 'em."

"Sure is a big deal about this drug thing. And the Michigan connection with the dealer. It's in the *Free Press* again today."

"Really has us on the map, doesn't it?"

"Have you ever met those lady agents?" Tom asked. "Or seen them around?"

"Never. You know, Rogue, I've talked to the D.E.A. guys out of Detroit and Chicago—they didn't have a clue about an investigation. When it went down, the guys in Detroit were given six hours notice."

"Strange. All engineered from somewhere else."

"I guess the F.B.I. knew they were flying into South Fox for some time. At least suspected it."

"Remember when they caught drug people back in '81 or '82? Wasn't a big deal, nothing like this. World's getting smaller."

"We're going out to Hog Island fishin' this spring, aren't we? Last year was great."

Shipman interrupted, "If I ever get ahead of everything. That's what I called you about. I want to talk to you. Got something bothering me. What about Friday night, dinner at the Blue Bird?"

"Fine with me."

"Seven?"

The Blue Bird Inn was loosely connected to the Early Bird. The Blue Bird was the town bar and connected to it was a formal dining room with large windows over looking a small river connecting Lake Leelanau and Lake Michigan. It was in the middle of town and, with the exception of the Early Bird, the Leland Mercantile, and the gas station, it was the only business open during the winter months. The dining room was open Thursday through Sunday, though patrons could eat in the bar all week. It opened after the Early Bird closed at two in the afternoon.

Tom met Walter Shipman as he got out of his car.

"Hi, Walter. What's up?"

"Good to see you, Rogue."

Shipman, the bigger man, put his arm over Tom's shoulder, and they shuffled into the dining room. The maitre d' knew both of them well and sat the two in a smoking area.

Shipman knew his friend begrudgingly accepted his bad habit and lit up immediately.

"Same old shit. I might just take up cigars again," Tom said, pretending to be serious, waving off the smoke.

"Buzz off! This is one of a few places where I can smoke anymore. County offices, smoke free. Mary Lou won't let me light up at home."

"Good for her! When did that start?" Tom asked.

"Over a year now." Shipman caught himself, remembering Mary Lou and Anne were best friends. It was Anne's death that ended Mary Lou's smoking.

"How you doing?" Shipman asked.

"All right, I guess. I think too much. Worry about nothing. The boys, their wives, the grandkids. They're doing great. I think about Anne. I'm not a good thinker *or* worrier."

They each had a drink. Tom always drank two vodka martinis before dinner and that ended it. Shipman was off-duty and drank a bourbon and water. They discussed Tom's successful food drive project; all thirteen service stations in the county giving free oil and filter changes on the Saturday before Christmas in exchange for canned goods for the needy. The results had been great for all five communities in the county and it had been reported in the *Charlevoix Courier*, fifty miles north.

"Are you busy enough, Rogue?"

"No", Tom answered.

"I've got something bothering me, and I don't have time for the legwork. I talked to Chief Forrest about it, mentioned you, and he gave me the go-ahead to ask you. If you wanted to do some work for us. Nothing real big."

"You're tight with the sheriff, aren't you?"

"Yes, we're close. He takes my advice," Shipman laughed.

"What's up?" Tom asked.

"Remember a guy drowning off North Fox. It was about the time of the drug deal."

"Yes, I think so." Tom did not recall much about it. "Did they find him?"

"No, never found the body. I was never real comfortable with it."

"Not finding him?" Tom asked.

"No, about the way it happened, twenty-five miles out in Lake Michigan in a ten-foot inflatable. Car parked at the ferry dock. Didn't go out to Beaver Island—least he didn't stay out there. He didn't own the raft, and he didn't borrow or rent it out there. Fact is, I don't think he rented it in Charlevoix."

"How do you know it wasn't his?"

"According to his son-in-law and wife he never owned a boat. Only took up fishing a few weeks before this happened. He had just retired. A bookkeeper."

"People do screwy things," Tom paused. "Why now? Think it's something to do with this drug thing?"

"That's what got me thinking. The guy was a bookkeeper for a Chrysler dealer. This guy Jack Leach is a Chrysler dealer. They were, what—Albion and Dewitt— sixty miles apart?" He shrugged his shoulders and looked at Tom. "Will you spend some time on this? I have your gas and phone and incidentals handled with Forrest."

"Jesus Christ," Tom laughed. "I'm retired. I'm not on the dole!" He wanted the work.

"I told Forrest you'd say something like that. We're hard up like everyone else, Rogue, but we've got you handled. If anything comes of this, you know, bigger expenses, we can discuss it. Will you do this for me?"

"Sure I'll help." He leaned forward in his chair. "I won't kid you, I'd about give my left arm to do anything."

Tom hesitated, then asked, "What is your feeling about this?"

"I don't know." Shaking his head, he said, "You know, I've got an imagination. It could be nothing. But could he have been involved? Could he have been murdered? Or could he have been part of it, seen it coming down, faked his death, hit the road?"

"What is his name?"

"Harry Jones."

"A white guy?"

"Hell, yes. Here, Rogue," Shipman went out to his car and returned with his attaché case.

"This is what I have. Not as much as I should have, but we thought it was a drowning. His family was satisfied it was a drowning, and that was it."

"I'll dig a little. See if anything comes of it." Tom said.

"All I ask is be low-keyed with your investigation. Present it as kind of a 'closing the books' procedure, if you would. I mean to the family... if you talk to them."

They each had another drink, ate dinner, talked of past experiences, planned for next summer's fishing trip, and agreed to be in contact on at least a twice-a-week basis. They parted with a "keep it low-keyed" and a wave from Walter Shipman.

Tom, almost trotting home, was excited about doing something, doing anything. He did not consider that Shipman may have been doing this for the sake of an old friend. Or if he did, he let it go quickly. Nor did he consider that a worried old friend might be covering the expenses, not Forrest and the county of Charlevoix.

The first thing Tom did when he got home was call the Coast Guard station in Frankfort, thirty miles south of Leland.

"Grant, this is Tom Morgan."

"The Rogue-man! How the hell are you?"

"As per usual. And your skinny ass?"

"Paintun' and chipun.' It's that time of year. Gonna ask me up to teach your power squadron class this spring?" Now the Coast Guardsman was putting Tom on. "Can't handle all those gals, can you?"

"You might get the call if you straighten up. All the *old* ladies have been asking about you. The *old,* old ladies."

"Hear you! And you talk about old?"

"I've a favor to ask Grant—take you two minutes," Tom said.

"No, my mother ain't available."

"Jesus, what a one-tracker."

Grant had Tom, and he knew it. Tom liked him though. Grant was always upbeat.

"What's up, Rogue?"

"Would you check last July's lake report? For the nineteenth, twentieth, and twenty-first."

"What you doing, planning last year's fishing trip?" asked Grant while he moved papers.

"Right… man, you guys must spend a lot of time alone!"

"Let's see, near shore, Frankfort to Charlevoix, including Grand Traverse Bay, it's the same all three days. Southwesterly wind to five knots, waves calm to two feet. We made a note—calm with fog patches. The weather buoy off Washington Island, Wisconsin, at 8:00 a.m., July nineteenth was calm. So I'd say the whole upper lake was about the same."

"See you, fart head. Say, I am going to call you when I give the squadron class this spring. So clean your uniform. And your act!"

"Thanks," Grant dropped the phone.

Tom wanted to make sure the raft had not just floated out into the lake after a near-shore mishap. He knew an inflatable could drift a long way in a short time with the right wind. But, if the wind were coming out of the southwest, it would not drift west, twenty miles out between North and South Fox islands. It would have been found on the shore. Maybe Shipman made that observation, but it wasn't in his notes.

From Shipman's notes, Tom entered his observations into a lap top computer:

7-21

1. On, 7-21, John Peltier, owner of commercial fishing boat, Janet E., found inflatable, partially submerged between N&S Fox Islands—noon.

2. That night, reported to sheriff deputy Freese—Beaver Island resident deputy. ID for a Harry Jones, 6310 Gibbs Road, Parma, MI, found in fishing box.

3. Reported (17:30) to sheriff office in Charlevoix. Spoke to det. W. Shipman.

4. Shipman contacted subject's wife, Alice Henrietta Jones, informed subj. fishing alone. Left on 7-20, -08:00- did not leave with boat. Subj. wife informed of situation. Contacted 7-21, 18:00.

5. 7-21, 18:30, Shipman contacted Coast Guard. USCG did fly-over 190-19:30, nothing spotted on N. Fox or area between Beaver.

6. 20:30, son-in-law, Henry Dunn, contacted desk sergeant Manthei; confirmed subj. didn't have boat—updated search. Subj. car '94 Dodge Stratus, dark gray, lic#4AA61.

7-22

1. Subj. car found (07:00) Beaver Island Ferry Dock—Charlevoix. C.G. called (07:30), informed subj. still missing. Will continue search later in a.m. Would recover inflatable from Beaver, bring to station in Charlevoix.

2. (08:45) son-in-law called, updated.

3. (10:15) Shipman inspected inflatable. No Mich. or other registration. Outboard 7 h.p.? Mercury left at sheriff field office—Beaver. 10' Achilles, appeared old, well-used. Stored at C.G. Charlevoix station.

Note: Ship remembered mentioning to C.G. officer on duty (?) strange that subj.—out there in inflatable—when it seemed he'd left from Charlevoix. 20-25 miles out. Like he really didn't know the lake.

4. (17:30) call Mrs. Jones—talked to son-in-law Dunn. Explained search, etc. Informed at this point presumed drowned.

5. Freese had called (about 15:15) talked to Harbor Master—Beaver—Glenallen. Remembered subj. Rented him boat (Steelcraft) twice, about 2-week period. Stayed at Erin Hotel. Freese checked Erin, had not stayed there week of drowning. Contacted locals—no one rented inflatable—fact no locals owned one.

7-24
1. Released car to son-in-law, also personal property.
2. Basically closed case. Missing, presumed drowned. No info suggests suicide.

That night in the study, feeling the fire, and drinking hot cocoa, Tom felt better about himself. Maybe it was just a small investigation and would be over in a hurry, but he was doing something. He would see if he could locate the inflatable and, if lucky, find its owner. That would take some time; he'd drive up to the Coast Guard station rather than call. He might drive downstate, interview Harry Jones' ex-employer, speak with his widow—just wrapping the case up, as Walter Shipman had suggested. That would take some time, also. He liked the idea. He hoped his sons would call; he'd tell them about the case he was on for another county. He wouldn't elaborate, just let them know that he was on board this drug thing. That he was a part of it.

When Anne was alive she often went to bed before Tom, leaving him by the fire. When he got into bed it was always warm. Sometimes, in the winter, now, he would place a hot pad on Anne's side before he went to bed, and when he got into bed, it would be warm and it would remind him of his wife. He would dream about her, but he never told anyone about that...This night he went to bed feeling happy and the heating pad didn't even occur to him.

The Coast Guard out-building, where the inflatable still remained, was as cold as the outside ten-degree weather. The young guardsman, who had just been introduced to Tom, pulled it down from a steel shelf and helped Tom unroll it. There was an identity plate on the inner left tube. Tom scribbled the numbers in his pad.

"Let's inflate it," Tom suggested.

"Yes, sir, I'll get a pump."

To Tom's surprise, both sections held air. He rolled it over, looking for a patch. He'd ask "Ship" about that and also check his notes.

"You ever see the motor?"

"No, sir. We talked about that once. Think it never came over from Beaver."

Tom talked briefly with the duty officer; they discussed the drug bust, and, in the conversation, the Coast Guardsman mentioned that Leach's boat was stored at Irish Marine, the big marina in town. Tom drove to Irish, introduced himself, and looked at the black boat stored inside. He'd seen a lot of sailboats, he thought, but that Hinckley with its shiny black hull, *that* was a boat. Using a ladder, he climbed into the cockpit. He saw what he was looking for near the bow of the boat—a large white plastic container, similar to a car-top luggage carrier.

He stepped forward, gingerly, and opened the container. A large inflatable was rolled inside. Tom laughed at himself, "You might as well shoot for the moon." Having forgotten his laptop, he hurried back to Leland. He called the U.S. home office of the inflatable company. The serial number Tom gave them was not on file. They were warranted for eight years, and the files had been purged. The lady sounded knowledge-able and said it probably was sold in '82 or '83, thirteen or fourteen years ago. Later, on the phone with Shipman, Shipman said that when he saw the raft the rear section was inflated and the front was flat. He'd wished he'd checked for the leak, but "if wishes were fishes." He believed the motor was left on the island, but Freese was still the resident deputy, and he'd welcome a call! Winters get long on Beaver Island.

Deputy Freese was busy watching soaps when Tom called. He was grumbling. The interference was bad. It was always scrambled that way when it blew out of the north-east. Plus they'd been poaching deer on the south end of the island. The D.N.R. had sent a guy over to find them and arrest the poachers; he was staying with Freese and was drunk all the time. Freese could not understand why the Department of Natural Resources would waste the money sending an agent out to the island to catch someone poach-ing deer. He knew there was poaching; he knew who did it, and he was certain it was for food, not for selling. There was a difference to him because he was a part of the island peo-ple and those who poached needed the food. It was the same with fishing. Freese was not considered by the islanders as an outsider. Tom listened and agreed.

"The motor was stolen, Tom. The day John Peltier brought it in. I thought Peltier took it, but he said no. Think it was a 7 h.p. Mercury. Looked in pretty good shape. Not new, but in good shape."

"Do you remember if the raft was fully inflated?"

"As I remember, the back was inflated and the front was flat."

"Did you look at it?"

"You mean close? No...," Freeze said.

"Any of the people out there knew this Harry Jones?"

"Peltier and Glenallen, the harbormaster, drank with him, I guess."

"Christ, they drink with everybody. Indian John even drinks with me."

Freese laughed. "Sometimes he probably doesn't even know it."

"I gotcha."

"I'll ask around, Tom. See if I can resurrect some memories. Do you think it's connected with that drug thing?"

"Naw, I think we're just closing it out."

Three days and one huge snowstorm later Tom was sitting in a car dealership in Albion, Michigan, interviewing Harry Jones' old employer.

"Harry was a gem, Mr. Morgan. A real gem. You know, he was in this building for over thirty years. With me and three other assholes just like me."

"I appreciate your honesty," Tom smiled, and they both laughed, breaking the tension.

"He was an accountant for you?" Tom asked.

"Bookkeeper here. He had two assistants and he ran the office."

"He paid the bills?"

"Payables, receivables—everything."

"Never a problem of any sort with him?"

"Oh, God, no. I have an external audit every couple of years. But you'd never need one with Harry."

"Did he have any friends in the business? Like other bookkeepers or dealers?"

"I don't think he had any friends, period. He was a loner. Hell, I once got him national press. Quoted in the *Washington Post* big time. And he was mad as hell at me."

The dealer told Tom the story leading Harry to his moment in the sun, at a dealer "think tank" seminar.

"And he was mad, for Christ's sake. Harry was a real loner. Didn't even have a hobby. I don't even know how good a friend he was to his wife. Have you met his wife?"

"Not yet."

"She's an artist. She's got her life; he *had* his."

"Christ, he must have done something."

"Harry was into stocks, bonds. That was his interest. Made some money at it too. If you ask me, I think it was work, dinner, CNN, and beddie bye."

"Ever heard of any big losses he took?"

"No, I might not have. He wasn't much of a talker. He made a lot of money on Chrysler stock. But I always thought he kinda sat on it. I wouldn't have even known about it except the check was delivered here. Goddamned near a million bucks!"

"Jesus, he was an investor."

"Myself, I had the feeling it was a one-shot deal."

"Why was that?" Tom asked.

"He retired soon after. I'd hinted about it. I had a girl here, lot younger, less money. I didn't tell him that, but I hinted. One Friday Harry just shook my hand, said he thought he'd retire, would give me two weeks notice but knew I didn't need it. And just walked out and went home."

"No hard feelings?"

"No hard feelings."

It had never occurred to the dealer there might be a connection between Harry Jones and the big drug deal involving the Chrysler dealer sixty miles north in Dewitt. The way this was going, it probably hadn't occurred to Tom Morgan, either. What it did occur to Morgan was the possibility of suicide. Could something have happened— investments gone bad, could he have snapped?

Tom shook hands with Mrs. Jones. She was cordial, reserved, yet he felt she liked him immediately. Her house was full of half-painted antique chests. She was in paint clothes, jeans, and a blue denim jacket over a turtleneck sweatshirt. He had interrupted her work, though she was expecting him. They were instantly involved in her paintings. Were they oils or acrylics? His wife had painted in watercolors; she had given summer classes in Glen Arbor. Mrs. Jones—now Alice Henrietta—was familiar with Glen Arbor and its art colony. Years ago she had taken a two-week course in sculpturing. That was a dream of hers. Doing a life-size sculpture. Was he familiar with Duane Hansen? Though she didn't do pop art, she loved his pop-influenced sculptures. Tom wasn't familiar with Duane Hansen or his sculptures. He asked if she did all of this herself, and she explained that she had assistants, actually associates, four of them, but that this was the off-season, and they were all out and about. She asked if his wife ever painted on wood, and he explained that she was dead, and that got him into the reason for his visit.

"This is," he started slowly, "what you might call a 'closing the books procedure.' That is why I came down to talk with you."

"Oh, I understand," Alice returned. "Completely."

They sat down, across from each other, at a dining room table crowded with tubes of paint and glass jars full of brushes. Tom and Alice drank decaffeinated coffee.

"Mr. Jones, before his death, wasn't having any financial stress was he?"

"Oh, my dear, no. Harry made a sizable profit through a stock transaction several years ago, and we put that entire thing in mutual funds. It has worked very well. You know, retirement had changed Harry so much. When I think back how he bloomed during those few months. It makes me both so happy and so sad. He was truly a changed person after he retired. From a person with little interests other than work."

"And he never had a hobby?"

"Nothing," she returned.

"Never?"

"Never. Isn't that amazing? Then one day he came in and proclaimed in front of my associates what his new plans were; first it was flying lessons, then fly-fishing."

"A fly-fisherman?"

"Yes, take fly-fishing lessons."

"Did he buy a fly rod?" Tom asked, pretending excitement over this venture.

"I didn't ever see it. He bought new clothes, though. Whole new wardrobe."

"Waders and such?"

"I never saw the waders. He said he was going up north and take lessons."

"There are good fly-fishing schools up north."

"He was so excited."

"He must have been, Alice. Getting new clothes and everything."

"His clothes were really for his new project."

"Another hobby?"

"You could say that. He rented an office in town, decorated it. Did his stock things there."

Alice leaned forward and touched Tom's arm, "Actually, a place to get away from me and all this work… and the ladies."

Tom laughed with Alice, and she poured a second cup of decaffeinated. Decaffeinated had a way with Tom. Sooner than later, he knew, he'd have to ask to use the bathroom. And he hated the thought.

"We still have his office. Harry took it on a two-year lease. If you'd like I'll show it to you. I think he was going to do stock work for others, maybe. He bought a word processor." She hesitated, "I don't think he ever got to use it."

"It sounds like Harry had plans for his retirement."

"I think most were just in Harry's mind, Mr. Morgan."

"Please, just call me Tom."

"Tom…."

"But retirement certainly changed him. It was a short, happy experience for Harry," she said, shaking her head. A tear started down from her eye; she caught it with the back of her hand. She smiled and Tom changed the subject.

"I'm just retired and things haven't blossomed for me." He stood. Smiling he said. "You, Alice, are the one that has done it! Look at all of the things around you—your art, your friends. I bet people really appreciate your art.

"You're appreciated," he continued, with a wide gesture of his arm. "What a lucky, ambitious person you are." His words quickly brought Alice out of her sad refection. Then he added, "And I would like to see the office."

"I'm going to give you the key and directions, Mr. Morgan, I'll stay here and work. I'm not dressed for town anyway."

She raced to get the key, her face still blushed from Tom's statement.

"Everything's as Harry left it. Feel free to snoop. Here is a picture of Harry, taken the week he retired. I don't think you have a picture. Take it, if you like."

Tom thanked her for the picture and slipped it into the folder he had carried with him. He told her he'd return the key after a visit to Harry's office. Spontaneously, without thought, Tom turned to Alice.

"Could I ask you out to dinner tonight?"

She shrugged, and with nothing else to say, she accepted.

"Yes, that would be a change," she said, "I'll make arrangements."

"Good. Eightish?"

"Eightish," she smiled.

He sucked it up, asked if he might use the bathroom before he left and quietly tried not to sound like a racehorse. As he was standing there he took out the picture of Harry Jones. The man looking back at him was unexpected. Square jawed, good looking, more like a television commentator than a Wally Peepers, bookkeeper type. He had a rugged, handsome, western look about him. From what he knew of Harry, Tom thought that trait was probably inherited; yet he knew you had to talk to a man, look into his eyes, to really know everything there was to know.

The office surprised Tom. It was not like Alice and her workplace. It was neat, well groomed, tastefully decorated. Sitting in Harry's chair, Tom thought the only thing it lacked was a fireplace. The room was warm. He thought it must share a common heat with the business below. He accessed the computer. There were stock quotes. There was what looked to Tom like various stock plans, amounts invested, but no names. There didn't appear to be any code names or references other than plan A, plan B, through to plan E. The stocks were mostly names of companies recognizable to Tom. There were legal pads in the desk, dozens of them, again with names of companies, arrows pointing, names scratched off, numbers with fractions. If all of it meant something, Tom knew it would take a mind other than his to figure it out. He noticed two empty pint bottles in the wastebasket. Somebody liked schnapps. He wondered if Harry was a drinker and who were his drinking friends. Inspecting the tall cabinet, he knew someone must have a taste for good liquor.

The two chairs across from the desk intrigued Tom. He must have been carrying on business with someone, he thought. There was a brown folder, boldly lettered "taxes" with a marker pen. He removed the papers. There were bills for the computer, the computer paper, receipts for the rent and the rental agreement.

In the folder there were also phone bills. Tom, sitting at the desk, studied them. There were few calls. Amazing for a business, he thought. There were two calls to Arlington, Virginia. He wrote the number and dates in his notepad. Then, on another page were repeated calls to Dewitt, Michigan. Same number, all different days. Tom was not particularly excitable, but he could feel the hair standing on the back of his neck. He tried the phone, but it was not in service. There were several calls to Beaver Island and two to Troy, Michigan; one a calling card from Beaver Island. He noted them carefully, not having a copy machine and not being sure he'd ever see them again. He locked the door. Then he made arrangements at a local motel. He had not planned to stay the night.

He picked Alice up at eight o'clock. She was in a full-length dress, dark blue, a necklace of small, single-band pearls; she carried a white handbag, smelled of Shalimir, exactly as Tom's wife use to smell.

"Hope I look all right for the occasion," Tom remarked.

"Oh, you look fine. I just felt like dressing."

They ate dinner at the English Inn, between Eaton Rapids and Lansing. It had been a Tudor mansion—darkly subdued, elegantly decorated, and quietly full of people. A pianist played in one corner of the main dining room.

Alice ordered a glass of wine, which instantly blushed her cheeks. She laughed about it, and he complimented her color. They talked about her current projects, her daughters, and his sons, and about how lucky they both had been surviving those years with a partner. Remarrying had never entered her mind. Actually, dating someone, as busy as she kept herself, had not even been considered. It was probably too soon anyway, she thought. Tom said that he hadn't considered either option, and he told Alice about Leland, and about how everyone felt it necessary to look after him, and that, in a small town like Leland, the church, the volunteer work, assisting at the marina, and fishing with his old friends kept him busy. He didn't mention the lonely winter nights by the fire while the wind howled over the lake and snow drifted so high that he'd barely get out beyond the coffee shop for days on end. It was much easier to laugh with Alice about her shows, her arts-and-crafts friends, and her work.

After dessert and a Bailey's for Alice and schnapps for Tom, they drove back to Alice's home. Both felt the drinks. Especially Alice.

"Would you come in, Tom? For a coffee."

"Sure... fine."

The drinks kept matters on a light side.

"I bet you've never had coffee served to you in such a burlesque style," Alice giggled, as coffee grounds scattered, coffee cups clinked, sugar and cream missed its mark, and dishtowels couldn't be found.

Why and how do things happen so quickly?

"This has been a nice evening, Tom." She stepped toward him and kissed him on the cheek.

He turned to her eyes and then kissed her on the lips. His hand, as large as a paw, or so it seemed to her, touched her back. She looked up, shut her eyes, held his arm, and kissed him back. It lasted a long moment. He started to say "could" when she said….

"Would you stay here tonight?"

"Could I?"

"I wish you would."

She then led him into her bedroom and pulled back the comforter.

"I'm going into the bathroom. I'll be back in a minute," she said.

She returned in a nightie, and he was standing in the darkened room in his shorts and tee shirt. She moved close to him and kissed him, nervously missing the side of his mouth.

"I'm really nervous," she murmured. "Really nervous."

"You can tell," he whispered, "I'm no pro at this myself."

She could feel him as he pulled her closer, hard and big, and she wondered if she could… how he would….

"Do you have a favorite side?" he asked.

"No, I'll get over here," she said, clawing at the other side of the bed.

They lay next to each other and he took off his shorts. She touched him, felt him, and she knew he was much larger than Harry, and wondered if she could accept him. They kissed; he fondled her breasts, thighs, and stomach and she inched under him. He was over her, and she was helping him into her, and as she became more fluid, he entered her. There was no rhythm to it, her legs weren't right to him, or to her, and it lasted for only seconds. He pulled himself out and away and over her, and they both lay flat in the bed, in the dark room. He breathed heavily.

"I'm sorry." Alice spoke, "I just wasn't ready, I guess."

"We were fine," He said, leaning over and kissing her.

They both lay awake in the bed, looking at the ceiling, saying nothing more. He knew she was awake. He would touch her hand, and she would instantly squeeze. Several hours went by, and he turned in the bed, toward her, and softly kissed her forehead. She inadvertently touched him, and he was hard. They kissed, and he touched her again as he had before, and this time she was more excited and less nervous. She pulled at him, and he was over her, entering her, and her legs were now gripping him firmly, and they were together in their lovemaking.

She awoke before sunrise and lay in bed and tried to get her thought process together. She had surprised herself. Now that's an understatement, she whispered to herself. She tried to resurrect the night. They had dinner, they drank, she knew she had been tipsy, they had laughed; and she knew he had admired her. She felt good about herself. She thought she looked good, and that she was appealing to him. And she wasn't afraid. Why not? She felt herself to be a modern woman in a new and different time. Hadn't she often said that to herself?

And here was this man next to her. He was nice, considerate, but smelled a little like Lava soap. She was next to a man she hardly knew. He was a quiet man, compassionate, she thought, but she really had no idea about him. She did not want to chance it that he might like to have sex again, and she didn't know exactly what she was going to say to him when he awoke, so she quietly got out of bed, dressed, and crept into the kitchen. She made coffee and icing-covered sweet rolls.

Later when Tom entered the kitchen there was not a touch of familiarity about him.

"Coffee?" she asked.

"Sure. Your sweet rolls smell great."

Like most women, Alice did not let issues surface and float and then wait and hope for something to happen. She just made issues happen. She poured coffee and sat down across from Tom.

"I'm more nervous this morning than I was last night. And I was plenty nervous last night. It is a cliché, I know, but we are," she said matter-of-factly, "consenting adults. Granted," she said, smiling, without hesitation, "a little light in the head. But... the dinner was great, the drinks were wonderful, and, well, the sex was good, too."

Tom looked at her. He quietly got up and refilled his coffee cup.

"Thanks for saying that, because I really didn't know what I was going to say this morning."

"Well," she returned, "at least you didn't sneak out of the house."

They both laughed.

Sitting among the chests and paints and brushes, he thought about inviting her to come see his place in Leland. He hesitated. He wasn't quite sure. Maybe this was the way it was supposed to end.

At the first pay phone he stopped, called the Dewitt number and got a disconnected message. He was ninety-nine percent sure, but just before turning west on I-96 from M-99, he stopped at a party store. Dewitt was in the Lansing directory, and, sure enough, the number was for the Jack Leach dealership. He remembered Walter Shipman talking about his imagination. He may have been closer to the truth than he realized.

Tom had no idea how Harry Jones could fit into the drug business with Jack Leach. The newspaper reports indicated how thorough the investigation had been before the indictments were presented, and, if Harry Jones were directly involved, Tom reasoned that the drug enforcement people would certainly have known about him. First, Tom would contact Shipman. He hoped this would not move beyond him. He wanted to be a part of this investigation. He even tried to figure a way to move further into this before telling Shipman what he had found, but short of a visit with Jack Leach in jail, he was stalled. Besides, that would be carrying his investigation a little too far.

The following day, over lunch, he discussed his findings with Shipman, who shook his head in amazement.

"Christ, Rogue! You working son-of-a-bitch. You stepped right up to this. Hell, this is something. What is your thinking?"

"I've followed this Leach thing in the papers. And you wonder why Jones would fit. Or, how he'd fit."

"Doesn't sound like the nature of the guy. You didn't talk to the son-in-law. You should contact him."

"God, I'm glad you said that," Tom said.

"What?"

"Me… I was hoping this didn't end it for me."

"Hell no. We're together on this. For our sake I'd like to carry it further. Don't know whether we can talk to Leach in jail. I can call some friends in the D.E.A., pick their brains. The dealership's closed, isn't it?"

"I called, phone's out."

"Maybe you could look around Dewitt. Find an ex-employee. Just see if they recognize Jones. You have a picture?"

"Yes." Tom handed the snapshot to Shipman.

"Nice looking guy." He studied it. "Really kind of a standout. Not how you would picture a bookkeeper. Looks quite important."

"Like me, huh?"

"No, like me!" Shipman tossed the photo back at his friend, and Tom grinned.

They agreed that Tom would check Leach's former employees and the son-in-law. Shipman would call the D.E.A.

people he knew, and Tom was headed back to Leland. He was feeling good about himself and his prospects. Tom knew Shipman was trying to score with this; that might keep him in the game.

"**I** remember him. He drove for us."

"Drove?"

"Yeah, fuckin' dealer trades. He'd pick up the cars Jack traded for."

"The ones with the drugs in them?"

"Right. With the drugs in them."

"Let me get this straight. He'd call in, see if you had a trade, then if you had one, he'd come in and drive for you?"

"Right."

"Did you know he lived near Albion?"

"Albion! Crazy fucker, cost him ten bucks just to drive back and forth."

"Right."

Tom had located the ex-sales-manager down the street from the closed dealership, selling on another dealer's used car lot.

"Do you think he was part of that?" he continued.

"Fuck, no! He was only around for a month or so. This thing went on for three or four years. You read the papers?" he said sarcastically.

The ex-sales-manager was trying to impress the other salesmen. Tom thought the change from sales-manager to used car salesman was probably too much for him to handle.

"What's up about this Jones?"

"He disappeared. Boating accident, we guess."

"Kind of a chippie little bastard. He up and quit. Unappreciative fucker."

"Leach never asked about him?"

"Matter of fact, he did. Came up and asked me what happened. Guess he thought I'd pissed him off. Asked me who he was a couple times. Hell, I don't know who the little fucker was; twenty-buck drivers come and go."

"Did Jones talk much to anyone else?"

"Only the mechanic's helper. He drove with him. He's down at the Shell station pumping gas."

Tom had an appointment to keep with the son-in-law, but he turned into the full-service gas station.

"Yeah, I remember him. Went on a couple buys with 'em. You know, drove him to pick up them drug cars," he smirked.

"Ever see him before he worked with you?"

"Nope never seen 'em."

"Ever ask about Jack Leach?"

"We talked about him."

"Remember what about?"

"You know, him being a good boss. Like, how he worked with us guys in the back end. You know, prepping the cars and trucks. I liked Mister Leach. I tell anybody who asks me that, you know."

Tom thanked the ex-mechanic's helper and drove to Jackson for a two o'clock appointment at the Big Boy with Henry Dunn, Harry's son-in-law. Dunn was standing in the doorway in a trench coat. He was short, stuffy, effeminate, a schoolteacher, and he welcomed the attention.

Shaking his head, he repeated, "Yes, I've always considered him kind of an odd ball. No hobbies, no friends really."

"Did well on the stock market," Tom added.

"I didn't know that. We didn't converse that much."

Tom's first reaction was that probably Harry Jones wasn't that much of an odd ball.

"I talked with your mother-in-law. Quite a lady."

"Yes, quite a work ethic."

"Did you see a change after he retired?"

"He avoided me. However, Martha—my wife—saw a remarkable change. As did my mother-in-law. I guess there was a new energy about him. Dashing about, new clothes, even a hobby... guess that's what got him into trouble." He paused, then blurted, "He even flew to Naples, Florida. God knows for what reason. Fishing, I guess."

"Alice Henrietta didn't mention it."

"One of his odd quirks." He hesitated. "She probably forgot. Strange, she never mentioned his doing well with stocks."

"She probably forgot."

"Yes," Henry considered.

Tom excused himself. He went to the pay phone and called Shipman.

"Didn't Jack Leach own a fancy condo in Naples," he asked.

After Shipman confirmed it, Tom returned to the table.

"How'd you find out he went to Naples?"

"Oh," Henry said, returning from deep thoughts about money. "Alice received mailers from the travel agency here in Jackson—frequent-flier applications, trip suggestions. She followed up on an excursion special, and the travel girl mentioned Harry's trip."

"She must have been floored."

"Yes and no. They were a different pair—he and the office, Alice and her crafts."

"Do you recall what travel agency?"

"Red Carpet, I believe."

"You've been a help, Henry. We're going to close this up. Mind if I give you a ring if I need anything?"

Henry nodded. "Hope I was helpful."

Tom stopped at the travel agency before his five-hour drive north. He wanted to know the dates of Jones' trip to

Naples. He identified himself. He noted the trip was exactly a month prior to his disappearance in Lake Michigan. Tom was confused about the dates, the trip, and the job at Jack Leach's dealership. He was anxious to share his day with Shipman.

Sitting in front of the fire late that evening he entered in his computer as much of the day's events as he remembered or had written on his notepad. The sales-manager thought Leach didn't know Jones. Jones was never seen at the dealership prior to his few weeks as a driver. Tom made a note to call Alice, see if she knew of his job as a driver. Then the trip to Naples. Jones hadn't mentioned it to Alice. If Jones had gone to Florida to see Jack Leach, what had happened at the dealership? Had he discovered something, was he blackmailing Leach? The tourist agency said they'd never done business with Jones before. Somehow, he'd ask Alice about it. He thought he could do it by phone without causing alarm.

The following evening he was to have dinner with Shipman at the Blue Bird. That morning he spoke briefly with Alice. She knew nothing about Harry and Jack Leach Chrysler. She was definite; she would have been surprised if he even set foot in a dealership again. When he retired, she said, he was so burned out with the business. She totally forgot Naples, but wasn't really surprised, though she didn't know Harry to keep things from her. She thought he might even have told her—while she was busy working with the girls. She wondered if Naples was known for its fishing. Tom couldn't help her on that. For the first time, Alice asked if something was amiss. Tom reassured her nothing was wrong. This uncomplicated person in her own non-violent world.

"A car jockey. Why that silly ass job?"

Neither Tom nor Shipman had an explanation.

"I'd like to talk to the Indian, Peltier, and Glenallen one of these days. See if they remember their conversations with Jones. I'll fly over when I'm sure they're on the island. And I've got to check out the rest of those phone numbers."

"I contacted the D.E.A. in Grand Rapids," Shipman said. "Couple guys I know real well. Funny, they were upbeat, said they'd get me some information. See if Leach could have had local help, more involvement, see if the case were still ongoing, or if it was closed. When they called back—I mean it was stone closed! Per their Washington office. Nothing handled locally—not even the federal prosecution. Not a chance in hell of talking with Jack Leach."

"That sounds strange. Where is he?"

"Grand Rapids. Strange isn't the word," he continued. "I know these guys well, Tom. And get this, not an hour later the under sheriff gets a call from somebody wondering if we ever recovered Jones' body. We haven't even been talking about it… Forrest, you, and me—that's it!"

"Well, as per usual, shit happens. And remember, I've been talking to people now."

"You're right." Shipman hesitated, "me and my imagination again!"

"You and your imagination have been clicking pretty good, old buddy."

Tom continued, "I'm off to Florida in a week. My yearly

trip to see mom, my sister, and the Miami boat show."

"You're a dreamer like me," Shipman laughed.

"Like I say, when my boat comes in, my boat will come in!"

"Buy Leach's. It'll be for sale."

"On my pension?" Tom laughed.

"What about a cottage on Beaver or a condo in Naples? Fire sale coming up! Tell me when you're leaving, Rogue, so I won't be bugging your answering service. Give me a number in Florida."

"I'll run over to Naples while I'm in Florida. See if I can find anyone who recognizes Harry Jones," Tom said.

"Meantime, I'll contact Leach's lawyer. He might be more cooperative about us speaking to him. If Leach is going to prison for twenty years on drugs, he's not admitting to murder, but if we could find a relationship of any kind."

"We're assuming a fluke, aren't we? A chance discovery, maybe blackmail—then ka-boom!"

"Can't assume anything," said Shipman. "It's a logical theory, though."

"If it weren't for that goofy two or three week job," Tom said, half talking to himself, "he still could have easily drowned—no thought of foul play at all."

"Still, it is one hell of a coincidence."

It was less of a coincidence when the two calls to Chrysler were traced to a Darrell Davey.

"Yes, Harry called me. Considered buying the dealership. Asked a few questions. I gave him encouragement. I wanted to set up a meeting, but he insisted on checking it out first.... Good guy, Harry. What a tragedy."

"Did he know Leach?"

"When he called me, I don't think he'd ever met him. I'm not quite sure."

"You knew Leach?"

"I had been his district manager once. It all kind of makes sense now... him not caring much about his car dealership."

In a way, Tom didn't feel good about what he had heard. That is, for the future of the investigation. Now there was a logical reason for Harry Jones' nosing around the dealership. Not really the way to buy a business though.... The blackmail theory was still plausible, but it was now more of a long shot. He would let Shipman try to make contact with Leach, and he would go to Florida, see his mother and sister, go to the boat show and dream. In fact, he was depressed. The third number he checked, the Arlington, Virginia number, was no longer in service.

Three days with this mother was plenty for Tom. His sister was ill, and he had two extra days before the flight back to Detroit. Nothing to do, he drove to Naples, although he'd lost interest in its importance. He thought Jones may well have gone to Florida to see Leach and discuss purchasing the dealership. He had the address of the condo. Surprised by how posh it was, he wondered how Jack Leach could acquire the boat, the place on Beaver Island and this without some red flag waving at the I.R.S. He would like to know how this whole drug scheme evolved, how it was discovered, and how it came down. He thought the two females must have been *some* agents; the persistence it must have taken doing most of the investigation themselves. He appreciated the D.E.A.'s silence, though Shipman hadn't. They had built a case to prosecute, and the trial hadn't begun. Someday, he thought, it would be nice to know how it all came down.

An elderly lady was approaching the condominium as Tom stood, arms akimbo, trying to decide if the apartment was really worth a million dollars. He figured he wasn't very far off. He removed his billfold to identify himself and politely called her Miss.

"Miss, my name is Tom Morgan."

"You are, let me guess, a police detective. I could say, 'not another one,' but I won't."

"Thanks for not hurting my feelings," Tom laughed. She was years younger than her age. She looked at his identification and at him.

"Come in for iced tea. You look harmless enough." Later seated, she said, "A detective from Leland, Michigan. Why, Mr. Morgan, aren't all criminals as nice as Mr. Leach? He was so accommodating."

"How long was he here?"

"Over four years, I believe. A nice wife—well-mannered, beautiful children. I think he would have liked to have retired here."

Tom said, "I'm sure he would. Especially right now."

Tom handed the photo of Harry Jones to the lady.

"I'm quite good with faces."

She studied the face for some time. "Looks exactly like Mr. Leach's brother. I only saw him once, but I'd swear it. It was amusing. He came up with the pest-control man. I thought *he* was a pest-control man," she laughed.

"You're quite sure this is the man?" She had returned the photo to Tom, and he handed it back.

"Yes, I'm sure."

"Did he tell you he was Jack Leach's brother?"

"No, he didn't. The pest-control man told me the next time he was in. He sprays monthly. He could possibly help you, too. His name is Robert. More tea?"

She continued as she poured, "This is decaffeinated."

Oh, boy, Tom thought.

"I should have guessed, though," she added. "He didn't leave with the pest-control truck."

"He stayed?"

"Yes, he stayed and talked with Miss Thurston. Mr. Leach wasn't down here."

"Thurston, the drug agent?" Tom responded. "Are you sure?"

"Yes. Of course, we didn't know that at the time. And shame on me, I actually thought it was a *friend* of Mr. Leach's."

"Did Jack talk about her?"

"Oh, no!" she exclaimed. "And I wouldn't mention it. They were never together. Actually, I'm not sure I saw Jack after that."

"Was she here often?"

"Only twice. She was standoffish. So beautiful on TV, though. And the other agent too."

"You're sure this man was Jack Leach's brother? I mean the man who said he was Jack Leach's brother?"

"It wasn't his brother was it?" She asked, scrutinizing Tom, as if she had been tricked.

"No it wasn't," Tom said.

"It *was* the man that was here, though," she added, in an uncompromising voice, looking again at the photo.

It was two and a half hours of anxious waiting at the pest-control office before Robert returned for the day. Tom had identified himself to the office manager. Robert was nervous. Yes, the photo was definitely Jack Leach's brother, and he had helped him spray that day. He was waiting for him in a white coat. Robert hadn't read about him in the papers, and wondered if he was part of the drug ring; everyone in the office agreed that he was. He hadn't a chance to look at the blond lady who walked into the apartment that day; he was busy leaving. But he was sure the guy in the photo was Jack Leach's brother. That he did know! At least he thought…. He didn't mention the hundred-dollar bill.

Invigorated by the discovery, Tom sped across Alligator Alley and had an upbeat fourth day with his eighty-six-year-old mother, lectures and all. He was anxious to return to Michigan. When he flew south he was afraid everything had returned to where it had started. Depressed, he thought it would take more than an imagination to resurrect any theories. Now it had turned again, and the confusion in his mind, as he flew north, excited him. The flight to Detroit, then to Traverse City, gave Tom time to think. He hoped he had asked the right questions and was as sure as he could be that Harry Jones had been in the company of one of the two drug agents.

Using his laptop, reviewing his notes, Tom was confused by the phone calls to Dewitt. A rush of calls one week, none the following week, then another week of daily calls. Why the blank period and where was Jones during this time? Not many options—the ex-sales manager, the ex-mechanic's helper, and maybe Alice Henrietta. He didn't want to call Alice. He doubted that she could relate the time, but more importantly, he was still uncertain about the two of them.

The following morning, the ex-sales manager, Alfred, told Tom the factory was going to reopen the dealership, in the interim until the trial, and that he was returning as a manager, that Chrysler was in the store now and if Tom would drive down, he, Tom, and the mechanic's helper could figure out, by the dealer trades, when Harry Jones worked. Four hours down, one hour in the store, four hours back, and Tom had his answer. The first week of calls were made before Harry Jones ever worked for Jack Leach Chrysler. And to the best of Alfred's recollection, there were no calls for an interview, no preemptive discussions whatsoever. He just walked into the showroom and asked for the job.

Tom called Shipman at home that night. Tom was flying to Beaver Island the following afternoon to talk with John Peltier and the harbormaster. He would have dinner with his friend in Charlevoix when he returned. He had a lot to discuss. Shipman said he had good and bad news. Jack Leach had been moved, for protective custody reasons, and that it would be difficult to arrange a meeting, but not impossible.

He, Shipman, had told the lawyer, who spoke with Leach, about an employee named Jones who had disappeared. After hearing the name, Leach had no reaction, couldn't even remember the name and would have no problem discussing it, but really didn't know what the hell it had to do with him. Evidently, at least at that moment, Jack Leach had more important matters on his mind than Harry Jones.

Tom Morgan was consumed with unanswered questions. At some point, after the hot cocoa, and before he fell asleep, he knew that he was destined to meet Camille Thurston.

During the night, he awoke from a restless sleep, thinking of Harry Jones, Jack Leach, and Camille. The uninterrupted eight days of calls would not leave Tom. Where was Harry during the week of no calls, before he went to work as a driver? He thought the answers might be on Beaver Island.

John Peltier was a bust. The lake was frozen over, and the fishing season had ended, and he was drinking heavily. He was vague with disinterest. He remembered drinking with the man in the photo—period! He did think the two of them had gone to the back of the Catholic Cemetery to see his brothers, but he wasn't sure of that. He might have gone alone; he went to see his brothers often, and it was usually after drinking at the Shamrock. Except he always went on Memorial Day. He only lit candles for his father and grandfather, but he always went to the cemetery for his brothers. He thanked Tom for lunch and excused himself to sit alone at a corner table. He thought he might go to the cemetery later that afternoon.

Glenallen was cheerful. Talking to someone new during the winter had that effect, especially if the person had flown to the island just to see him. He started the conversation with a corny fishing joke and the bartender said, "Jesus, Glenallen, what the fuck!" Tom knew the harbormaster slightly, and the harbormaster knew Tom. He had a good mind, remembering Tom and his friend Shipman had fished the small islands for bass. The conversation soon centered around the drug bust, as it would for years to come. The two female agents had been there to see Jack Leach's cottage and to ask questions. They were like TV stars now, like movie actresses to the islanders. Glenallen had talked to them, and he would never forget it.

"Did they ever mention Harry Jones?" Tom asked Glenallen.

"Never came up in the conversation. But, I remember him. Nice guy. Loaned him my truck. Got him a boat a couple times. New to fishing—didn't know whether his ass was drilled or reamed, though. Never caught fish one. You don't think he was in that drug deal, do you?"

"Don't know."

"His death was weird, wasn't it?"

"You mean being out there in a dingy?"

"Yeah—." Glenallen paused. "You know, Shipman asked me if he got it here."

"And you told him—?"

"None of the natives even have an inflatable. He wasn't out here then anyway." After a second, he continued. "You know, I kept telling him to stay in close."

"How do you think he got out there?"

"Goddamned if I know. Cannot believe the son-of-a-bitch motored out from Charlevoix. It's twenty-some fuckin' miles!" He drew out the words. "Nice guy—quiet," he continued. "Loved that schnapps."

Funny, Tom thought, no one else had mentioned his drinking.

Tom asked, "Did he ever mention Jack Leach. Refer to him at all?"

"Only what a beauty his boat was. Surprised—like me—Leach having a boat like that, leaving it sit out here and having the house too. I guess we understand that now," Glenallen said, hitting Tom on the arm and laughing. His laugh amused Tom. Once it got started Tom thought it sounded like a train engine. They both ended up laughing over nothing.

Glenallen, leaning back in his chair, did remember, "You know, he did ask me once if that Leach spent Christmas's here. Thought that kind of funny."

"Why? A few summer people do fly up."

"Yes, I know. He just hadn't asked any particular question about anyone else up here. It stuck out."

"Remember what you told him?" Tom asked.

"Yes… I told him no. Fact was, he was thinking about trucking his boat to Florida."

"Did you tell him where in Florida?"

"Hell, I don't know, can't remember any specifics. I might have cause Leach told me once or twice he had a place in Naples."

"And that was about it?"

"About it," Glenallen replied.

"Anyone at the Erin?"

"Stu is around." Looking out the window, he said, "Yeah, he's over there."

Tom walked across the street. Stuart, real estate broker, hotel entrepreneur, was sitting at the desk reading a real estate brochure.

"Property really going up," he said as Tom entered. "Everyone trying to get away."

Tom introduced himself and asked if he had a register for the past summer. Two file cabinets later and a lot of shuffling produced the results Tom had expected, or at least hoped, to find. Jones had registered at the Erin Hotel on the same day as the last of the eight calls. He stayed two nights. Later, with some shoveling, Tom and Glenallen pushed their way into the harbormaster's office. It was closed for the winter and as cold inside as out. Jack Leach docked the same day Harry Jones left the island. Later that day, Tom learned that Harry had flown off after Leach had arrived. There must have been a connection, Tom thought. Glenallen had no records, but as he recalled, it was Jones' second visit to the island, and the last time he ever saw Harry Jones. On both occasions he had rented a boat from Glenallen.

Flying back to Charlevoix, the distance between North Fox and Beaver didn't look so great, but it was damned hard for Tom to believe someone would motor on an inflatable all the way from Charlevoix to that area between those islands.

At the Weathervane restaurant that evening, Tom and Shipman reviewed everything Tom had done since flying to Florida, including the earlier, depressing conversation with Darrell Davey of Chrysler. Shipman was incredibly upbeat. He called Forrest, the sheriff, at home. He insisted Tom stay at his house and the following morning he, Forrest, and Tom spent four hours discussing the entire investigation. Shipman discussed the D.E.A.'s lack of cooperation. Forrest was mad, seemed driven, but not optimistic about cooperation. He'd run into their lack of cooperation before. More time was needed to sort everything out. Forrest was high on Tom's idea of interviewing Thurston, would look into it, but again, lacked much enthusiasm for results. He might work through the F.B.I. on that one, he said. As Tom told Shipman later, over a drink, the sheriff looked to have "blood in his eye." He was excited. He thought this whole thing was about to get turned up a notch or two.

The next day Tom talked with one of his sons. He had wanted to tell them what he was doing; in fact, he could hardly contain himself. Tom said as much as he could; his son sounded surprised—thrilled, actually. When Tom hung up, he was consumed with excitement, because he knew before bedtime he'd be getting a call from son number two. And sure enough it happened. Tom detected an awe in his son's voice. He was excited for his father. He had to hear the story again that he'd already heard from his brother. He asked his father question upon question; they were on the phone for thirty minutes. God, your grandchildren will *not* believe this, Dad. Dad, they will not *believe this*! And the '*Dad*' had never, ever sounded so full to Tom. When he finally hung up the phone that night, tears had already come from his eyes. His nose began to water, and he cried aloud. This was the best part of it all for Tom Morgan.

T wo days later, Walter Shipman, Tom Morgan, Jack Leach, and Jack Leach's lawyer sat at a small table in a windowless room inside the federal prison in Milan, Michigan. Jack Leach, clean-shaven, in a tank suit, looked well-rested, more alive than pictures Tom had seen of him on TV, when he was being led from his home in Dewitt. He smiled at Tom and Walter. He was attempting to plea bargain, turn state's witness; screws were turning, according to the news reports. People were in custody everywhere—Toronto, New York, Washington, Texas, Mexico. Some were still fugitives. Leach's lawyer, partner in a high-profile law firm in Miami, had postured brilliantly for his client on news TV; Leach was only a courier, not a dealer, not a "biggie" in the drug case.

"We are only going to discuss a Mr. Harry Jones here, today, gentlemen. Agreed?" The lawyer asked.

Both Tom and Walter nodded their heads. Walter leaned forward, notebook in hand. His library glasses, which Tom had not seen before, made him look surreal, more like a professor than a detective. Of course the lawyer from Miami had seen it all.

"Excuse me in advance if I interrupt you," the lawyer said.

"That's quite alright," Shipman said, looking up at the lawyer.

"How well do you know Harry Jones?" Shipman asked Leach.

"I don't know Harry Jones. I didn't know him a year ago. I didn't know him six months ago. And I don't know him now," Leach said.

"He worked for you once, didn't he?"

"He was a driver, not an employee. Casual labor. He'd go on dealer trades—the sales-manager would toss him twenty bucks."

"The cars with the drugs in them," Walter added.

"Gentlemen!" the lawyer demanded harshly.

"You never saw him on Beaver Island?"

"Never!" Leach said.

"Ever on Fox Island?"

"Never!"

"But you saw him in Dewitt?"

"Once, maybe twice. The closest I came to him was one night I was working late; he came in, said he lost his billfold. We looked for it. Couldn't find it. He left."

"Were you suspicious of him?"

"I was suspicious of everyone."

"Why?"

"Why, because I was transporting drugs. Wouldn't you be?"

"Did you talk to Harry Jones before he went to work for you?"

"Never."

"He made eight calls to your dealership a week before you hired him." Shipman said.

"Never, ever talked to him."

"Somebody talked to him eight times. How was he hired?"

"Probably hired off the street. I didn't personally hire him to drive cars. I had a salesmanager for that."

"Eight phone calls?"

"Not to get *that* job. Yeah, like I said, he was there a week, two at the most. Never saw him before, never afterward."

After a pause, with no further questions from Walter, Tom held up a finger. "May I ask a question?"

"Have at it," Leach responded sarcastically.

"What were you doing that night when Jones came in?"

"Paperwork, I suppose," he shrugged his shoulder unconvincingly.

"He didn't see you with drugs, did he?"

There was a momentary pause in Leach's response. What thoughts claimed his mind only he and perhaps his lawyer knew.

"Am I asking too difficult a question? If he did see you—?"

"No, he did not," Leach shot back.

The inference was planted. Leach's lawyer stood up. He expected to play this visit positively, as a portrayal of his client as a helpful ex-employer, interested in the tragedy of a drowning, only a fringe player in the deeper, darker world of international drug trade.

"That's it, gentlemen!"

The detectives rose and thanked both men for the opportunity to interview Mr. Leach. Driving north, both now thought it likely Harry Jones had interrupted Leach while involved in his second profession. But other questions haunted both of them. Why would he have gone all the way to Florida if he wanted to speak to the D.E.A. people? How would he have known the agent Thurston? If he had tipped off the D.E.A., and it was her case, why in the hell wouldn't she meet him someplace in Michigan—where the incident occurred? And what about the harbormaster's account of Jones's interest in Jack Leach up on Beaver Island. They both agreed that could have been coincidental. But the relationship with Leach?

"That son-of-a-bitch wasn't out on Beaver Island fishing."

"When did this big interest in fishing begin anyway?"

"After he retired, I think. Maybe June. I'll have to check my 'Alice' comments," Tom stated.

"Before he went to the dealership, before Naples?" Shipman hesitated. He drew a cigarette from somewhere in his sport jacket and lit it, all in one motion. He cracked the window for Tom's sake, and blew from a deep drag.

"There's not a chance in hell this guy could still be alive, is there?"

"Oh, Jesus, Ship!"

Tom interrupted himself. "Somehow I gotta talk to that Thurston. Somehow, goddamnit! This is nuts! You'd think she'd at least discuss it. What with the drowning and everything. Wouldn't affect their case. Might make a stronger case against Leach." He paused, "Hell, maybe they don't want a stronger case. Maybe they know something already. Who the fuck knows. Wouldn't think they'd want the F.B.I. involved. Damnit, will Forrest let me try to contact her? Or the other agent?"

The answer came sooner than Tom expected. Shipman dropped Tom in Cadillac, where they had met for the trip down state to the prison. The sheriff, anxious to hear about the interview with Leach, had called his detective at home. Shipman called Tom. During the conversation, Forrest mentioned he'd talked to a F.B.I. friend in Grand Rapids, who told him Camille Thurston was no longer in the D.E.A. She was still active in the case, but retired and teaching law in South Dakota. He believed it was at a state university.

"What if I make contact with her now?" Tom asked.

"Let me talk to Forrest. I bet you'll pay hell getting anything out of her. Especially right now."

"Where there's a will, there's a way."

"Rogue, you're an optimist."

"As per usual, Walter."

It took two phone calls. The University of South Dakota in Vermilion. The switchboard operator knew Miss Thurston immediately; Thurston was teaching two first-year law courses in criminal law and torts, plus a general course in business law in the School of Business. To Tom it looked like a twelve-hour trip. Interstate 80 through Illinois and Iowa, north on U.S. 29 another ninety miles. He saw no reason why Forrest would disagree with the chance for an interview.

Tom didn't understand how the mechanics of an agency like the D.E.A. operated. If they had moles, assuming Harry Jones was a mole, and if they were discovered or murdered or disappeared, was there ever an acknowledgment to the unsuspecting family? Or would the D.E.A. take a passive approach, hoping their involvement was never discovered? Are families ever paid off, a disclaimer signed, in hopes that *Sixty Minutes* never finds out? It didn't seem plausible in a society like ours. Yet he had just finished reading Peter Matthiessen's, *In the Spirit of Crazy Horse*, and, by God, he really wondered. Indian movements were sure as hell a lot less critical to the national psyche during the nineteen seventies than the drug problem is today. Hell, the drug issue even then was of greater consequence. And look what happened as far as the F.B.I. and the Bureau of Indian Affairs were concerned. Even with a law enforcement mentality, if he actually had one, there was an underlying fear of what authority could do when it was so disposed. Then there was the bad-guy problem, the balancing act, how much you had to give to get, and the realization that it had to go against the bad guy at whatever cost. That is how we make peace with it Tom guessed. In his uneasiness, he made peace with it that way, too.

Tom didn't know any bad officers. First hand, he didn't know many bad criminals. When you're an officer in a community that had seen only one murder in twenty-some years, and not a very gruesome one at that, you don't see many bad on either side. Tom figured bad criminals made bad officers. He could have been partial on that theory, however.

"Good luck, Tom," Forrest said over the phone. "Remember, you're in official capacity." Forrest had never felt one hundred percent about Tom. It was a matter of control. Tom wasn't one of his men. He was, however, amazed at Tom's performance and had congratulated Shipman on his choice.

Vermilion, South Dakota. It was a main-street, college town that sat on a high bluff overlooking the Missouri River and its valley. The town had once been below the bluff, along the river, but a giant flood cleared the town, and it was moved up on the bluff. That was over a hundred years ago. The valley was six miles wide and, beyond the valley and the river, were the hills of Nebraska. The school of seven thousand was bigger than the town. It was a quiet, isolated place, fifty miles from the nearest big city. It had a good feeling about it. It felt solid. Tom thought it must be a great place to be involved in education. Sitting in his room in the Super 8 Motel, he still hadn't a plan to meet and interview Camille Thurston. He knew that she lived alone in a recently acquired Italianate mansion on Austin Avenue, and he knew the hours she taught and the buildings she taught in, even the approximate location of her office in the law school. But under no circumstances did he want a flat no, a quick refusal to meet him, and an empty trip back to Michigan. So he knew he wouldn't phone her. And knocking at her residence might startle her and be too intimidating. That left one choice.

Tom poked his head around the door of her classroom, as the students hustled through into the high-walled, noisy hallway of the old law building. She was gathering her papers.

"Hi," he said. "Miss Thurston?"

She turned to him, casually indifferent. She was wearing glasses.

"Just a sec," she returned. "I've a train of thought I need to keep on track."

He walked into the room, without a note pad, empty handed, except for a jacket over his arm, and seated himself directly in front of her. Now with his jacket over a knee, he looked up at Camille Thurston. Except for newspapers, he had only seen her once and that was on television. Her stature was anything but diminished by the reality of her presence. Her blond hair, pulled straight back into a twist, accentuated her high cheekbones and strong jaw. Her face and figure struck him as bigger than life.

As if unaware, she studied the ceiling, then jotted notes on a legal pad. He felt nervous and thought he wasn't hiding it well. Slightly intimidated, he continued to stare, and she glanced down at him, and he smiled and she said,

"You're amused. I see a twinkle."

"No, I was only thinking how you really do look bigger than life."

"Is that a compliment?" She asked, writing.

"It's meant to be. I remember the first time I saw a picture of Alan Ladd. He was in a crowd—rather than riding high in a western. Couldn't have been five-foot-six. And Stallone, hardly the heavyweight I imagined in *Rocky*."

He added, "I don't meet many celebrities."

Immediately he knew—by a sudden dark look—that "celebrity" wasn't taken as a compliment. She turned her attention to him and he said, "I'm Tom Morgan. I drove out from Michigan to speak with you."

"Wish you had called me," she returned passively, putting her papers, a book, and several legal pads under her arm.

"I was afraid if I called you wouldn't speak to me."

"You were probably right, Mr. Morgan."

She sat abruptly, arms still full, with a look of a short, terse statement.

"Reporters have been a bother here. It has affected my work," she said impatiently.

What Tom did not want was his next words coming on top of a negative. But he had no choice.

"I'm not a reporter. I'm a detective. From a little village of five hundred people—Leland, Michigan."

Camille started to speak, but Tom continued, "I'm only trying to close out a situation in our town."

"If it has *anything, anything*," she repeated sternly, "to do with the drug case, I have nothing to say. You know it hasn't come to trial yet," she lectured. "You know I can't talk about it. So you know I'm sorry, but you've made a long trip for nothing."

She stood up, put her books down, walked to a coat-stand, put on her coat hurriedly, and walked back toward the desk, never looking at the seated detective.

"It is not about a drug case. It has nothing to do with the drug case."

He looked up at her as she picked up her papers and book. She paused, looking down at him. "What does it have to do with, then?"

"It has to do with a drowning. I just need to put an end to it," he added.

"What would I know about a drowning? A drowning in—where did you say?"

"Leland, Michigan."

"In Leland, Michigan."

"That's why I just wanted to ask you a couple of questions." Tom was not pleading, but he was close. Again she paused. She removed her glasses, sticking them into her coat pocket. She looked down into his eyes as he continued to look at her. After a moment she beckoned with her head.

"Come with me. We'll go into my office."

"Thanks," he said as he stood up to follow.

Her office was as small as his study. It was well organized and looked freshly painted. Facing east, it was bright with sunlight. It overlooked the tennis courts. She took his coat and hung it under hers on a coat-rack as old as the building. She pulled up one of the two chairs that were against the wall and motioned for him to sit down.

"Where are you staying?"

"Super 8."

"Not exactly the Ritz Carlton," she said.

"No. But I imagine you love it out here."

"I love it, and the people. And the town." She stood up, "I'm getting a cup of coffee. Want one?"

"Yes, thanks."

He felt a slight change from the first few minutes with her. Maybe she felt sorry for him driving the distance. Maybe she was curious enough to hear him out. Maybe, he thought, she was picking *his* brain. She returned with two Styrofoam cups.

"Hope you like decaf."

Then she turned serious. "You'll excuse my abruptness; my caution. The press has been unrelenting—to Victoria and me. Her position and, well, her job privacy, has given her an advantage. I don't have that advantage here on a college campus."

"Are they still bothering you?" Tom asked.

"I should get a percentage at the Super 8."

Tom noticed that Camille never laughed; she only smiled. She continued, "Actually, it's slowed. Besides, most people make an advance contact. Give me a chance to say no," she winked at him. "I don't like them coming to my home." She turned her swivel chair, looking beyond the window. Shaking her head, she sighed, "And it's going to be a huge, long trial." Turning to him, she said, "Now, what about this drowning?"

"A Harry Jones. A retired bookkeeper. He drowned, or rather he disappeared, presumed drowned, north of North Fox Island on Lake Michigan. The island is part of Leelanau County. Leland is the county seat. See this," he turned the back of his left hand to her, pointing to the nail of his little finger, "That's us in Michigan." Tom knew she had been in Michigan.

"And?"

"Did you know Harry Jones?"

"Should I?"

"Did he work for you?"

"As an agent?"

"Any way?"

"Didn't know a Harry Jones. I've never known an agent named Harry Jones. Never had a friend named Harry Jones."

"A mole named Harry Jones?"

"Never a mole named Harry Jones."

There was not a blink of an eye. Not so much as a twitch. He had looked her square in the eyes because this was his chance, and there was nothing.

"I see you've finished your decaf, Tom. Another cup?"

She stood to get both more coffee. He stood up.

"It goes through me like a bolt of lightning," he said.

She smiled. "Down the hall on the left." She followed him out of the office, acknowledging several students as she left. Standing at the urinal, six inches from the white tile, his thinking became blurred, even his vision. It could have been the cracked tile doing it to him, or the relief from the decaf, but he thought it was his excitement. She was confident. Confident enough to insist on another cup of coffee and leave herself open to more questions. Her investigative skills were still intact. He felt if he missed something, she would probably speak to him again. But now, over a second coffee, he would carry it further.

"This is Harry Jones," he said, handing Camille the photo. She didn't study it. "I thought you just might recall something, seeing him somewhere. May look younger than he is—was," he corrected himself.

"He was retired," he continued.

"Looks too young to be retired. Body never recovered. Why is that? Bodies usually float, don't they?"

He thought she would know the answer to that question.

"Water's too cold. When a body sinks to the bottom it's too cold for bacteria to work. So there is no decaying. It doesn't bloat, so it just lies on the bottom. If the warming effect ever really happens, bodies will be popping up all over the place."

He said it as a joke, but she didn't smile. "I thought you might have recognized him," Tom said, taking back the picture and putting it in his shirt pocket. "Because he was in your company in Naples, Florida."

Some people can ask a question with a blank stare, and that is what Tom Morgan did.

"Must have been in a crowd, Tom. I don't recognize him," she said, pulling back her chair. "You really do go to some lengths to close a drowning."

"When you have only one murder in your county in twenty-nine years, you've got the time."

"And of course, this is a missing person's case."

"About Naples," Tom returned. There was a pause. "Supposedly it was just you and Harry Jones in Jack Leach's apartment."

Camille stood up. "That is an incorrect supposition, Mr. Morgan. An incorrect supposition. And remember what I said about the drug case. It just can't be discussed."

Tom stood up. Neither smiled, and Tom shook her hand. She had a strong handshake, like that of a good salesman.

"I think I've covered what I wanted to ask," Tom said. "But if I missed something, would you mind if I call? I'll be going back to Michigan in the morning."

"I don't see any problem with that. If I'm in—not busy. Remember what I said about the drug case though."

When Tom returned to his room and his laptop, he didn't have much to enter, and he thought he had seen the last he'd see of Camille Thurston.

I t was four-thirty Washington time when Victoria Nelson answered the call from Camille at her office in the Drug Enforcement Administration building. They talked briefly. She would call Cami back from her apartment as soon as she got home. She was concerned with the composure of

Cami's voice, or the lack thereof.

"Better yet, go to Whimp's for dinner," Victoria said. "I'll call you there at eight. And, Cami, keep him there another day. Let me check things a little—a Tom Morgan from Leland."

Later that evening the phone rang at the Super 8. It was Camille Thurston.

"Have lunch with me tomorrow. If you can stay an extra day."

"Yes - I can handle the twenty-six a night, I guess."

"You've driven seven hundred miles for a ten minute conversation. I owe you at least that."

"I appreciate it, Miss Thurston."

"I've a ten o'clock tomorrow," she said. "Let's say I pick you up at eleven forty-five, OK?"

"Fine," he said.

Tom wondered, after his strained departure, what had come over her. He was convinced the old lady and the pest-control man both couldn't be wrong about Harry Jones. And everyone had seen her face on television. She didn't deny being in Naples either. He was sure the conversation would return to Harry Jones.

Whimp's Steakhouse was crowded for a Wednesday night—college students, professors, town folks, farmers, and cattlemen. The town of Burbank, on the "Bottoms," five miles east of Vermillion had a population of twenty-six people, and Whimp's was a typical, South Dakota, farm community restaurant. Grubby and weather-beaten on the outside, the bar connected to the dining room—overly noisy, but family-owned and operated with great food and big servings.

Camille was eating alone when the call arrived. She had to back into the kitchen to hear Victoria over the phone.

"Tom Morgan an older guy?"

"Yes," Camille shouted.

RETIRED

"He's retired. Working with a neighboring sheriff department. Closing out the drowning. Low-keyed, backwoods background. I'm surprised he went out to South Dakota."

"He went to Naples, Florida. Saw people who identified Jones with me in Leach's condo. Why was I ever there investigating when he showed up? What a lousy coincidence."

"That's over. Don't worry about it, Cami. Morgan, he has probably read too many detective novels. Be nice to him, hear him out. Sounds like he'll tell you whatever he knows. I won't call you back. I'll see you next weekend. Call me back if you feel like it, though. Love you!"

She finished her meal. People came to her table until she beckoned a fellow professor to the table for a beer. A nice guy who had introduced her around the campus when she first arrived. Later in the fall he wanted to take her goose hunting on the sand flats out in the Missouri River. A great sport and wonderful sunsets, he said. She was game.

Camille was in front of the Super 8 at exactly eleven forty-five.

"Nice of you to do this, Miss Thurston."

"Cami, Tom. Everyone everywhere calls me Cami."

She pulled a cigarette from a pack on the console and lit it.

"Hope you don't mind if I smoke."

"Your car, your lungs."

"Sounds like my father, *and* my mother, *and* my brother, *and*—say, I brought a lunch. I'm going to show you why I love this place so much."

She drove east from town along the bluff and turned into a cemetery of old oaks and maples. She stopped at the edge of the bluff—a panoramic view of the valley, across to Nebraska and north and south as far as one could see. The hills of Nebraska were blue in the morning sun. The colors were blue and gray and grayish white. She opened her window, inhaling the cold morning air.

"I come here often—just to get away. Beautiful cemetery, isn't it? Did you notice there is no new part to it?" She hesitated, then she said, "And I don't know a soul in it."

"So quiet and personal. What a wonderful place it must be in the summer," Tom remarked. Then he added, "You *do* feel like you should just know someone."

"I'm from the Midwest," she exclaimed.

"I think I read that."

"Clinton, Iowa. On the Mississippi."

"Why did you get into the D.E.A.?"

"Met Victoria. She was from New York. Roomed together as freshmen at Penn State. She was studying criminology. I got the bug listening to her talk about it."

"What were you studying?"

"Shit, nothing. I was a jock on a scholarship."

"When did you study law?"

"That was after I was in the agency. In Washington. Did you go into law enforcement from college?"

"Hell, no, right from the army. I got a degree years later. One semester hour at a time," Tom laughed.

"In criminal justice?"

"No, business. I had big dreams like everyone. They didn't have criminal justice in Traverse City, anyway."

"Like law enforcement?"

He nodded.

"It was different for me, though. In Leland being a cop is a community project as much as being a crime stopper."

"Sounds perfect to me."

"Sounds like your early experiences weren't that great."

"Nasty," she inhaled, blowing the smoke from her window. "Lots of good female agents never made it. People that would be good for the agency now. People like Victoria."

"You two stuck it out."

"It was because we were together—our relationship made it last. And we fought the sexist shit hard, but that's past history now."

"You two always worked together?"

"Mostly. Never the best assignments. Some supervisors were better than others. A few looked out for us. Lot of desk crap, though. Cleanup stuff. After the jobs. After the good ones were solved."

She turned to Tom, "We'd have never gotten the big case if anyone thought it would have turned like it did. We got lucky early on that one."

"Lucky, but you were good, too."

"The connection had already been made between North Fox Island and the east coast. We caught it in a memo. But no one could work it back from there. We asked and the supervisor gave us the go. That's how it started. Backing it up from North Fox was the big problem. Once we got it to the source, the payoffs to the factory people down there, and to the Mexican government people, it fell into place quite easily. Then all the dominoes started to fall.

"You taped Leach early on?"

"Can't talk about that, friend."

"Lot of competition in the department?"

"Sure, a lot between agencies, too. The F.B.I., A.T.F., C.I.A., all of them fighting. Funding is a big part of it." She changed the subject. "You know, this chicken I brought has gotten cold. We'll go to my place. I'll heat it up." She turned the Cherokee around, and they left the cemetery. "I cheated. I got the chicken at the carryout. I've this feeling when you buy chicken in the morning at a carryout, you might be getting last night's redones."

She heated the chicken and placed it between them on a small marble table in the living room.

"You've furnished this all yourself?" Tom asked admiring her home.

"The downstairs, yes. Vic helped. A lot of antiquing to do upstairs, though. God it cost! Collecting this stuff. I'm trying to stick to the period."

All this time Tom felt she had something else on her mind. Then she either ran out of talk or was tired of it.

"I don't like to see Leach and this plea-bargaining stuff. I don't like to see him get out of this thing so lightly."

"Other, bigger fish," Tom answered.

"Sure, but he was no courier. Jesus, a nine hundred thousand condo in Florida, half-a-million dollar boat, joint on Beaver Island—and God knows how much to keep that dealership afloat. Not right, Tom. Too much work, too much risk for that." Cami said.

"It is your baby."

"Not anymore," she returned, loudly. Aggravated, she stood, "I'm you, you know. I'm the cop. I get 'em behind bars, but I don't make the judgment call on who's more important than who. Who goes down harder than the next guy. That's all politics and bullshit."

"I agree."

"So let the bastard plea-bargain. Fine—then after he's plea bargained, ratted on everybody, spring this Harry Jones drowning thing on him, and bang, nobody is going to give him short time. No government protection program there."

"We're talking as cops, and I don't know the legality."

"It's legal, Tom Morgan. Believe me it's legal. It's just got to seem straight up. The timing I mean."

"You mean when we decide it's a possible murder, and we carry through with it."

"That's right." She paused, then sat down across from him. "*What* do you think?"

"About the timing?" He had not kept pace with her.

"No… what do you think really happened, out there on Lake Michigan?"

She riveted into him with her eyes. He backed away, his shoulders and arms first. He paused.

"I guess I believe Harry Jones discovered that Jack Leach

car dealer was Jack Leach, drug-runner. He found out what was going on and basically got murdered. Blackmail could have been involved. But I don't think so. Nothing in Harry's past leads that way. What worries me… Cami." He paused, then he moved in, "What bothers me is the time problem, and dates and phone calls. And places like Naples. I'm no expert on this, but it adds up to me that he was working for you. Or, at least, he was telling you things. And he goes out and gets himself killed for you and your agency. And poof! Nothing from you. Nothing from anybody."

He shook his head, "I don't know how it works, and I don't claim to, but if I'm right, or just a little right, god-damnit, things should have been said; wrongs made right. At least a recognition for his family's sake. You know," he stared, instructing Cami now, "telling them he was a part of it. Even—however small—that something could have happened because of it."

Cami stood up. He did not look up at her face, but she turned around and walked to the bay window. She remained there.

She thought to herself that he's in a world of his own, this small-town detective. Leland must be a wonderful place to have that perception of law and order and justice.

"That is your theory, Tom?" She asked, looking into the early afternoon.

"Yes, I believe it is," he softly responded.

"I mean *your* theory?"

"Yes, my theory. I'm the only one working on this. I've discussed it with another detective in Charlevoix. But I didn't explain it like I just did to you."

"You explained your theory very well. An A plus, Mr. Tom."

She turned around and stared at him; he reminded her of someone, but she couldn't recall who. "I'll take you back. I've a faculty meeting at four. It needs some preparation."

In the five-minute ride back to the motel they talked of spring and of her father and of her father's farm, and in their conversation, his wife Anne came up, and they talked about her death. She left him with a handshake and a smile. He never saw her again. That night he wished he were home in his own warm bed. He thought of Anne and of Alice Henrietta Jones.

Camille did not call Victoria back. In fact, she waited for her to come to Vermillion. Victoria visited her friend once a month, flying either to Sioux Falls or Sioux City, Iowa. She always rented a car at the airport. This time Cami met her at the airport, and they drove back together. In the hour's drive from Sioux City, they discussed everything that was said between Cami and Tom Morgan.

That evening they ate lightly and tried to forget Harry Jones and Tom Morgan. Cami had set two places for them in the large dining room. She was going to serve dinner in the atrium, but she felt this was more private. She had romantically placed candles throughout the first floor of the house when she decorated. Now they were lit. She knew how much Victoria liked them.

"We're having my college freshman dinner number one tonight, Vic." She spoke with a smile, struggling. She served two small chicken potpies and a salad.

"The wine is a plus."

"At least you're not sitting them on the Spode china tonight."

Cami smiled. She had always been able to laugh with Victoria.

"Eighty-five-cent pot pies on Spode, that's class to me," Cami said.

"Remember after finals once, we bought two bottles of cheap champagne and got crazy drinking champagne and eating hot onion rolls and butter."

"We did that after the drug thing went public too." Cami said solemnly.

They were standing, holding hands, and Victoria pulled Cami's arm firmly. Cami was having a hard time breaking from the interview with Tom Morgan.

Victoria looked into her eyes.

"Remember, we did this for us. It was for our personal freedom," she whispered. "But we did it for the agency too. It's salvation. For our country, for God's sake. This damned war on drugs. But more than all that, Cami, it was for a freedom for all of us." She gestured to herself, then to Cami. "It has made us, you and me, and working women everywhere free to do whatever we want in this world. Free to pursue our professions without the breaking and halting and interfering of sexism. And the damned harassment. Freedom to be the best at what we're good at—not just a freedom in the workplace, either. I hear about this, what we did for women in every walk of life. I," she paused…, "we felt it—worse. It was the profession. But we've all felt it whatever any of us did. There were terrible sacrifices made. Think of the gals that left us, and the A.T.F.! Harassed out of their chosen profession. Only because they were women, for Christ's sake." Lighting a cigarette she added, "And the other sacrifices. The Harry Joneses of the world." She paused and there was silence. Victoria knew that she was just giving a speech, that it was a make-no-sense, lousy speech, that the timing wasn't right, that it was not getting to the point and that it was not fair, her friend bearing the brunt of this inquiry. Cami sat down. Motionless, she looked beyond the candle in front of her.

Victoria seated herself across from Cami, interfering with her gaze, and the thoughts that went beyond.

Victoria continued, not pleading for acceptance, "Yes, the other sacrifice. Harry Jones. We had to do this. We couldn't share that triumph—to make it work like it did. If we'd shared it at all, even the tinniest bit, they'd have made him as big as us. Maybe bigger, with his age and his every-man appeal. This freedom of ours would never have come about. Not now, anyway. The hero shit, that role meant nothing to me except as a vehicle. But we couldn't have shared it and made it work."

She hesitated, looking into Cami's eyes; looking for any recognition. Cami took Victoria's cigarette and inhaled. She stood, searching for her own cigarettes. Smoking now, she moved toward the open glass doorway to the atrium.

"Did we really need Harry Jones?" She pleaded.

"He found the missing link." Victoria paused. "Hindsight? Somehow we'd have discovered it. It wasn't him I underestimated, Cami," Victoria said defensively, though softly. "It was his age, his vitality. His overwhelming energy. Like he had rediscovered life and was fighting for every moment of it. When I met him in the Catskills, he was different than the man I had met earlier. After he told his story, what he had found and how he had done it, I think I panicked. I began to visualize this as his case... not ours! I was seeing him as the dominant figure in this case." She paused, "That wasn't going to happen. That couldn't happen. It just couldn't."

"Was he taking control?" Cami asked.

Victoria thought about the word "control." She would never admit that she thought of losing control, not even to Cami.

"I was intimidated, yes."

She continued, "After I read that crazy story in the auto news, when I first found him, I thought he was our man—an expert. A naive kind of an expert in the car dealer business who would be manageable. I thought he'd be slower at it, more timid, I'd prod him along into finding something—then take over. But he caught onto the whole damned thing so quickly. Ran beyond me. And then we were there, and he'd done it all. Found the whole thing himself."

She turned to Cami. "I know the man," Victoria hammered, loudly. "He was going to be a part of it. Period."

She sighed and exhaled. "I'll never feel that way about older people again. My attitude toward senior agents, older agents, older anyone, has turned 180 degrees." There was a long pause, a deafening silence. For a split moment neither knew how close or far away they were from the other. Then, Victoria stood up and walked to her friend and, saying nothing, took Cami's hand and lead her upstairs to the bedroom.

They undressed quietly, Cami in front, with her back to Victoria. Victoria stood close behind her, then held her hands, both with their arms down beside their bodies, touching. Victoria kissed the side of her neck and moved to her upper back. Cami felt the goose bumps rising on her neck. She moved down the small of her back with her lips and sometimes her tongue. She knelt on one knee behind Cami and pulled down her panties, and Cami still in heels, stepped out of them. Victoria touched Cami's buttocks with her cheek and mouth, and moved back up her back, now feeling her hips and waist with her open hands. She undid Cami's bra, taking it from her shoulders and letting it fall on the floor quietly. There was only the hum of the forced air through the vents breaking the silence. She cupped the palms of her hands around Cami's breast, and massaged her nipples with the two first fingers of each hand, and Cami, now breathing loudly, shook ever so slightly. She let Victoria lead her to the bed, and, stepping out of her heels, lay on her back, pulling her friend down beside her. Now on her side and over her, Victoria kissed her friend's forehead, her cheek, and her lips. Her hand moved from Cami's heaving breast to her stomach and then below to her moving body. She had lifted her knees and her legs opened and now Victoria's hand was part of her movement, and her finger was now in her and the motion violent, and Cami whimpered and spoke softly, urging herself and Victoria's hand on, and then she climaxed. Her body continued to move slowly for only a short time. She closed her eyes and was soon asleep. Victoria covered her friends warm body with a sheet. She watched her and listened, and when she was asleep, Victoria masturbated. Then she went to sleep.

Later, during the night and closer to morning, Cami awoke and quietly went into the bathroom and showered. When she returned Victoria was standing, waiting for her. They made love again, exactly as they had earlier. Except this time, when it was over, Victoria put her arm around Cami's shoulder and told her how much she loved her.

"This is the way it had to happen," she said. "The way we did it. It had to be done that way to free us. To make us what we are now and what all of us will be." Cami didn't speak, but in the darkness, with her moments of thought, her feelings of self doubt had disappeared. She knew she had walked away from that life. She had walked away from it by a conscious choice, and she was happy with that choice, but she didn't want to be reminded why she walked.

In the early spring, Camille Thurston sat watching the evening news. The big drug trial had begun, and it was the news. The car dealer suspect from Michigan, the one who had "named names," was now being questioned and under suspicion in the disappearance and possible murder near Beaver Island, Michigan, of an innocent, unsuspecting retiree who just happened into the drug scene. The dealer's lawyer—from Miami—was outraged. He had successfully plea-bargained for his client. The lawyer, on national TV, stated that Jack Leach, his client, had literally given the government its case. Now this monstrous double-cross, as he called it. He was furious, wondering aloud, how the government would ever again get anyone to turn for the "state," for the people's case.

The reports that followed credited a retired detective from Michigan—working on his own, often at his own expense—with much of the investigation that led to this revelation.

Camille called Tom Morgan at his home in Leland and complimented him. He was drinking hot cocoa when the phone rang, and he told her she was damned lucky to get through because his sons had called, after they saw the TV news, and the local news media had already found out who the detective was. His phone was ringing constantly. He told Cami he might just walk down to the marina to get away from it all. He asked her if she'd stopped smoking, and she laughed. Actually laughed, Tom thought. Her house was coming well. Her job was great, and she would like to see him again. He felt good when she hung up. He strolled down to the marina and walked among the boats and the boaters. No one knew him, yet.

Victoria called Cami that night. She felt that it was time to give credit to the right people now. But she never felt she was wrong about the drug case and what she had done.

One morning, during the summer of that year, Tom walked into the Early Bird for breakfast. Around the big table. He ordered breakfast, then remembered he'd forgotten to buy the Detroit paper at the coin machine. He went back out, got the paper, and started to sit down when he caught the picture of Cami Thurston on the front page. He turned the paper over at the fold and read: "Agent killed in South Dakota accident." He rose from the table and moved to a single booth. His friends looked at Tom. He started to read further, then got up and left. He did not reply when a friend shouted, "Something wrong, Tom?"

He walked quickly across the street, up past the stores now beginning to open, and to his house on the lake. He closed the door behind him and placed the paper—open—on the dining room table. Now in slow motion he made coffee and standing over the paper he read the article about Camille Thurston. A semi-truck, loaded with livestock for slaughter in Sioux City, had blown a tire; the driver lost control, swerving into the median. It rolled over, crashing into Camille's oncoming car, apparently killing her instantly. She was going to Sioux Falls for the day, antique hunting. He choked over his coffee as tears came to his face. He sat down in his study, his head in his hands, and cried.

That afternoon he tried to reach Victoria Nelson in Arlington, but failed. He contacted the university and the switchboard operator told Tom that memorial services were to be held in the Baptist Church and that her ashes were to be scattered in the cemetery on the bluff in Vermillion.

Before the memorial service, the minister introduced several people to the congregation, including her closest friend, Victoria Nelson. Victoria had driven to South Dakota from her apartment in Arlington, knowing that the long drive by herself was the only way she could mourn her friend's death alone. The minister also mentioned a Thomas Morgan, of

Leland, Michigan, who would not be there. He had written a short remembrance that the minister would read later; it spoke of their cemetery and about a single soul that was in it. Sharing grief with others was not an act for everyone.

Victoria remained at the cemetery alone that evening. It had been a special place for the two of them. Neither had ever talked about death, though. It was always about their future. Each needed her space, but it was always about their lives together in the future. She didn't stay in Cami's home and did not return to it.

Victoria started back late the following morning. She made one last trip to the cemetery, with the valley, the river, and the blue hills of Nebraska beyond it. It had rained that morning, and the colors were green, and white, and grayish white. She stopped in Amana, Iowa, that night. The following afternoon, driving on Interstate 80 through Illinois and into Indiana, she slowed and thought for several moments. Then she turned off the interstate onto Highway 99 and drove toward Albion, Michigan, sixty miles to the north.

She felt a need to stop and speak to the widow of Harry Jones.

PART **THREE**

Leland. Tom Morgan had not intended to be an important person, even in Leland. All he ever wanted was to be a hero to his sons. The hero business had gotten beyond him; he was now on the Memorial Day, Fourth of July, and Labor Day planning boards. Chairman of the Community Fund Drive. He was forever downplaying his role in the drug case. His friends thought it was quiet modesty speaking; for himself, he felt that after a short period, a more balanced perspective would prevail, though in his heart he knew small-town heroes last forever. A contentment should have set in for Tom. At the big table in the Early Bird his opinion was sought on practically every subject. Then, during the long summer afternoons, he would help at the marina, docking and fueling boats, sharing his knowledge of the local waters. He loved the boats and the boat people. He was one of them. If things got too hectic, though, he just went fishing.

Life, however, would not be quite that simple. He had just returned from a two-day fishing trip with Walter

Shipman. One of those Michigan fishing trips… a break in the weather, a high sky, a calm lake, and gone from the world. They had fished the quiet bays of Garden Island, north of Beaver where the smallmouth bass feeding among the rocks and the coon-tails were hitting. He was slightly miffed that Walter's catch had been better, attributing it to the fact that, in the spirit of sportsmanship, he had let his friend sit in the front chair of the boat, allowing for better casting vision. But the two days were wonderful, and the weather was perfect. They were good friends, and the two nights at the Erin, dinners at the Lodge, and drinks at the Shamrock were a good time for both. In retrospect, though, a small encounter and a short conversation in the Shamrock should have foretold an event soon to unravel before Tom Morgan.

While entering St. James Harbor, after the second day of fishing, John Peltier's trawler, below a sky of frenzied gulls, motored past. While John and his Indian companion waved, a third man in a mackinaw turned his back, busying himself among the gill nets heaped on the aft deck.

"With the ice going out early," Walter commented, "John must be having a good year."

Later at the Shamrock, in passing, Tom had spoken to the Indian fisherman, who was fast approaching drunkenness,

"Was a good summer…." Peltier hiccupped.

"New crew?" Tom asked.

"One is. Got rid of the other," he slurred.

"Took on another transplant?"

"Might say that," said John, smiling and winking at the two.

He laughed, teetered sideways, hiccupped again, and grabbed his way through the crowd to the door. "Transplanted from the depths of the sea—this new one, gents."

"What the hell was he talking about?" Walter asked.

"Goddamned if I know."

But who in the middle of the night at the Shamrock Bar was looking for double meanings.

Tom had just unpacked his fishing gear, thrown his clothes in the washer, and settled into a rocker on the porch with a cup of cocoa. Breathing in the cool southwesterly now coming in from Lake Michigan, he felt relaxed. Then the doorbell rang. When he opened the door a bearded man, about five-ten, who he had never seen, stood before him.

"Tom Morgan?"

"Yes, how can I help you?"

"My name is Harry Jones."

"Pardon me?" his head turned obliquely in disbelief. He faked a smile.

"I'm Harry Jones."

Tom took a half-step backward. "You're a crackpot. Who are you?"

"Believe me," the man resounded sternly. He put his hand up, palm facing Tom, as if to calm him. "Just believe me. Let me speak to you."

He stepped inside, letting the screen hit hard against the casing. Tom took another step backward, but said confidently, "You can stop right there!"

"Ask me anything you know about me. I'll answer you."

"Where'd you get that inflatable?" Tom shot back, the first thing to come to his mind.

"Inflatable? What inflatable? What are you talking about?"

"The boat you were in. The boat they found. You're a crackpot, that's what you are. You don't know what an inflatable is?"

"Yes I do." He acted confused.

"A boat you blow up with air, right," Tom said sarcastically.

"Jesus, I don't know what you're talking about."

Tom started to grab his arm.

"I can't leave here," Harry said. "They're after me and you've got to help me."

The plea stopped Tom. "You know who I am?"

"Yes, You're Tom Morgan the investigator. You've been working my death!"

The remark nailed Tom right between the eyes. Knowing he was a policeman, Tom thought, he'd have to be crazy barging into his house, approaching him like this. Eyeballing the intruder, Tom asked, "Who's trying to kill you?"

"Laura—Victoria Nelson."

"And the whole Drug Enforcement Administration is after you I suppose?"

"Victoria for sure."

"Why Victoria Nelson?"

"Goddamned if I know. I gave her the whole case."

"The drug case?" Tom responded, not really asking a question.

"Yes, the drug case—Jack Leach, North Fox, the whole thing."

"I'll tell you what," Tom interrupted. "I don't know you, I don't recognize you, and I don't want to know you. You don't look like Harry Jones to me through that beard." He paused. "I've got an electric razor. You're going to shave. Then I'm going to feel better or worse about you. I've a picture of Harry Jones... clean-shaven."

Tom wasn't sure, but this man didn't appear uncomfortably wacky. He didn't have the snapshot that Alice Henrietta had given him, but he was sure Harry Jones would be recognizable to him. He left the man standing in the hall, then returning, handing him the razor; he continued his questioning.

"Where have you been? You haven't been hiding at your home. And, incidentally, where is your home?"

"Albion. And, no, Alice thinks I'm dead. I've been with John, the fisherman on Beaver Island all this time."

"Wait," Tom said, grabbing back the razor, "John Peltier? With John Peltier all this time?" The remark John had made at the Shamrock flew past Tom.

"He saved me," the stranger said, shaking his head. "Pulled me from the water. After she'd pushed me in... left me for a goner. I was in bad shape. He and his mother saved my life. I know that *he* saved my life. Here...." He pulled a beaded necklace from around his neck. "This is John's."

Tom took it, then handed it back. He felt embarrassed for the man.

"I'm going up to see John tomorrow," Tom stated. "And you're going in the can 'til I get back."

"You can't do that," he shouted. "I swear to you, Damnit, she tried to kill me. If you take me into a jail, she'll find out." He hesitated, then took up the story. "I was in bad shape. It took awhile to get the whole thing back. First, I thought the two of them were in with Leach. Then I saw them on John's TV, an interview they did. I don't know what's going on, but I swear Victoria Nelson tried to kill me. I'll stay at your house, wait for you. When I have your confidence, somehow we've got to find out what's happening."

"I'm going to Beaver Island to see John. That is for sure!"

"You know what?" Wearily, the stranger sat down in a chair by a small desk that held a telephone. "I'm tired, dead tired. My back is killing me. And I feel a hundred years old tonight. Maybe it's the excitement—that I'm finally doing something about all of this. I want to lie down somewhere, go to sleep. Just rest for awhile. Anywhere. I've been sleeping on a floor mattress... it seems like forever.

His helplessness caught Tom.

"No," Tom said, waving it off. "There's a shower upstairs. And a bed you can sleep in."

The man went upstairs. Tom re-heated his cocoa, then changed his mind. He took a water glass from the cupboard, poured it half full of bourbon, half water, and sat down in the rocker on the screened porch. He didn't hear the boaters in the marina, their muted conversation and laughter only several hundred feet away, nor did he notice the breeze blowing in from the big lake. It was too nice a night, Tom thought. Too Goddamned serene for this! After a full swallow, he quietly said aloud, "What in the hell is happening to me?"

He was awake most of the night, either in the rocker, at the kitchen table, or just standing, looking into the darkness of the lake. There were questions he asked, and answers he wanted now, but each time he got to the bottom of the stairs he could hear his guest sleeping and he let it go. On one of his first trips into the kitchen, he noticed the man's billfold placed in the center of the table. He had left it there for a reason. Why hadn't Tom asked? In the first minutes, he had never thought of asking to see the man's driver's license. He sat down at the kitchen table, opened the billfold, and there was Harry Jones' Michigan driver's license, his picture in the lower left corner. He had pulled it out of the plastic holder for Tom. Tom was spooked. He studied it closely and was not sure if it was the man upstairs. But the more he recalled their earlier conversation, the more he wanted to believe....

At one point during the night he considered phoning Walter Shipman. "Guess what, Walter, I've got a man sleeping in my upstairs bedroom who say's he's Harry Jones. What do you think of that?" He got damned close to making that call, wanted to, but he didn't, and, the more he thought, the more he convinced himself not to involve anyone else. Other involvement could come later.

At 4:30 a.m. he dialed John Peltier's number on Beaver Island, and it was as if John had been waiting for the call.

"I knew you'd call when Harry got there," he said abruptly.

"Is he Harry Jones?"

"He's Harry Jones all right."

"Then you knew he was coming?"

"I got 'em the ride."

"I want to speak to you in person."

"You can speak to me. But that man is Harry Jones."

"When will you be back from fishing?"

"If you come today, I'll wait. I knew this call would happen."

It was the way he carefully picked each word that froze Tom to the receiver. "You people need proof; you need witnesses. I know how you work. Just be careful with old Harry—he's been through it. Gonna fly up? Call me when you get here, I'll pick you up."

It sounded like he was dragging on a cigarette as he closed down the phone. Tom didn't expect John Peltier to understand the need for corroborating evidence, or more importantly, at least at this stage, the real need for Tom's psyche to adjust to the current truth. He knew that in a short time he was going to learn a lot about truth from the fisherman on Beaver Island.

They sat in John's cabin in the woods. It was little more than a shack covered with tarpaper held tight with fir stripping. Only one room saw sunlight. It was full of hanging plants. It was an addition constructed by boxing in discarded four-foot wooden storm windows on three rows of cinder block foundation, joined with two-by-fours at the roofline. They were sealed with duct tape to make it wind-proof. The place smelled of boiled cabbage, smoked fish, and marijuana. In the living room, where they sat, was a new three-piece set of furniture covered in paisley. His mother, who he introduced as Marilyn, and the Indian helper sat on the davenport. They looked at Tom and John as they spoke, but never said a word.

"When I picked him out of the water, he was almost gone. His head half under, his one arm locked around the tube of the dingy—a death grip like I've never seen. His muscles had gone rigid. If it weren't for it being a rubber boat, I'd 'a had to break his arm. He looked up at me, but he wasn't really there. He says, 'God. God oh God, she's trying to kill me.' Looked up at me like I was God. Didn't know what he was talking about."

He paused for a moment, then self-consciously looked at the two on the davenport, then back at Tom.

"I told him, 'I'm not God, I'm the fisherman from the Shamrock.' I'd met him in the Shamrock." There was another pause. "He was almost gone," John said.

"How long do you think he was in the water?" Tom asked.

"Not long. Long enough to kill a man. We've talked about it, me and Kenny," he nodded to the Indian on the paisley davenport who nodded back.

"We picked this boat up on radar. Maybe an hour earlier. It was foggy—patchy. Fog movin' like clouds if you were in it, then you were out. We'd been workin' around the south end of Beaver. Had nets off High Island. I was watchin' this boat on the screen. She was sittin', thought she was trolling, was about to blast a warning when she started moving. Seemed to circle, like she was lost in the fog. She circled, widening her circle, then she stopped. Probably broke out of the fog bank, oriented herself. Saw where they were, then broke for the mainland."

"Heading east?"

"Yes. Toward Charlevoix or Petoskey."

"Ever see the boat?"

"Never saw her. Was a good two miles off. We was working, doing two, three knots. And Harry…? Probably in the water an hour.'Cause that's where we found him. Right where she was, the boat he was on, no question. There was nobody else out there."

"You don't think Harry was in the rubber boat?"

"Shit, no, he wasn't in that dingy. They planted it, and he just got lucky. Fog cleared, he spotted it. He was just god-damned lucky is what he was. They'd inflated that boat 'cause the front valve wasn't tight—was leaking air."

"Does he remember all that?"

"Not all of it. He's still getting parts of it back. You know, he was unconscious, partly conscious, or out of it for days."

"That is probably why he didn't remember the inflatable."

"When we got him in the boat his pulse was shit. His fingers were purple, his toes purple. We used Kenny's sleeping bag. He keeps it on the boat—so when he's too drunk to walk home." He laughed and nodded to Kenny, and Kenny nodded back with a smile.

"We took off his clothes, put him in the sleeping bag. He was as stiff as a board. Kenny got in with him, but he was so cold Kenny couldn't last long. Kenny took the helm, then I crawled in… his pulse was fuckin' nothin'. As we got in the harbor he came around—just a little. He was all fucked up, confused, tried to fight us. Was scared shitless. Kept telling us not to tell anyone. No one, he said. Then he stopped fighting, and said, 'Help me, just help me,' and he was out."

"You didn't know him very well?" Tom asked.

"I knew him from the Shamrock. He was a good man… went with me to see my brothers in the cemetery. Didn't even know me, but went with me. We talked about God. That's where I talk about God."

"Good a place as any," Tom agreed.

There was a pause. Marilyn had a blank look on her face and Kenny nodded.

"First off," John continued, "I knew I should tell someone, after turning in the dingy, and them thinking he drowned. I knew someone should know, but he'd come around remembering, telling me to help him and hide him, and he'd plead with me, and when I was gone he'd ask Marilyn to help him. 'Will you help me till I get better,' he would say." John shrugged his shoulders, "So I helped him, and I hid him."

"How long did it take for him to come around?"

"A long time. Cause he was weak, would get a fever. Had to watch out for a fever. We've been through this before. Lots of Indians die from this; my father, my uncles. They call it a cold death, this hypothermia. White people always think Indians drink themselves to death. Because their kidneys were gone, they always said they drank themselves to death. But old people get cold easy. They're always cold. On reservations their houses never get warm. They get pneumonia, go into shock, and their kidneys fail them. They don't all die old drunks, they die from being cold." He hesitated. His mother had given each of them a cup of coffee, and she refilled the cups without asking.

"Young people can handle the cold, old people can't. Real young can't either. Marilyn saved lots of people when she lived on the reservation. She knows how to do it. When the old people get cold their color changes as pale as the gray sky, their pulse goes down and they have to be warmed slow. Slowly, maybe a degree an hour. Blankets. Layers of blankets. No liquor. No sweat lodges. Warm water enemas. Over and over… to save their kidneys. Marilyn knows how to save people."

"That is how you saved Harry?"

"Just that way. Harry's a tough old fighter, though. There's a strength about him," John added. "Wonder if he always had that?"

"I don't know him. Only through other people," Tom added. "He's always been a dead man to me."

"You got to help him on this, Tom Morgan. You're the only one. He thought hard about this. We felt it had to be you 'cause you're a part of the drug thing, but still you're outside of it. An outsider, right?"

"Right."

"That's how he feels about you."

"Did he remember this Victoria to you, the drug agent?"

"Hell, he said she was a lady who paid him to find her daughter. He was all screwed up till he saw her on my TV, recognized her, then he was really screwed up. I tried to help him understand in my way, but Jesus Christ, an Indian fisherman on Beaver Island! What the hell did I know about those people. After I told him I'd gone to see his wife, he got mad as hell, told me to just protect him—nothin' more. Got mad as hell."

"You saw Alice Henrietta?"

"I figured the 'she' who tried to kill him might have been his wife. I went to visit her. I knew in five minutes that lady had no part in any of this."

"You didn't tell her about Harry being here alive?"

"Oh, shit, no." He stood up, irritated by the question. "For Christ's sake, I was an 'old friend.' You take me for some fuckin' idiot?"

"I just asked. You got to remember I never met Harry Jones in my life. To me the guy is dead, and he knocks on my door. 'I'm Harry Jones, how are you tonight.'"

John laughed. It seemed to lighten the mood. Marilyn and the helper both laughed. John sat down and lit a hand-rolled joint. He gave one to Marilyn and Kenny, and they both lit up, all three sitting in the living room smoking marijuana. They didn't offer one to Tom but he figured they must have concluded that he was a friend.

"Funny thing," John continued. "Wasn't a short time after I visited his wife but a Coast Guard buddy called me from Charlevoix. Said they were going to board me looking for drugs. This zero tolerance shit. I work with these men all the time, in search and rescues out here. Said it was an order from the D.E.A. Sure 'nough, two days and up comes a rescue boat, boards me, looks for nothing, but wants to know the names of my crew and who and how many I got. I'd left Harry here since the warning, and that son-of-a-bitch wasn't about drugs. It was about Harry. I know damned well."

"Wonder who else visited Alice Henrietta?" Tom asked, then stood up. "This is one day I'll never forget." He looked at John. "This is you and me and Harry on the Q.T. Nobody else, we're promising each other that. We'll talk as this goes along. Harry will stay with me while we plot this thing out. I didn't talk to him enough last night to know what he remembers, what he doesn't. He was tired."

"Yeah, he tires easy, but I think he's fine. I've been watchin', I've been listening to him. I think the Coast Guard business was it—what made him say now was the time to get goin' with his life again." He hesitated, "I'd say you two got a job ahead of you."

Tom returned home late that evening. Harry Jones was sitting in the study reading a newspaper. Tom sat down across from him.

"Convinced?" Harry didn't look up from the paper as he turned the page.

"I had to do that."

"I know you did...wanted you to. But are you convinced?"

"Sorry about last night." Tom said.

"Just so we are on the same plane," Harry said, putting down the paper.

"You're goddamn lucky, Harry."

"Now three of us know that."

"You'll stay here. Better hang on to the beard. No one should recognize you. Frankly," Tom added with a smile, "from your license, I'm still not a hundred percent." He heated cocoa for the two of them.

"Tell me something about yourself."

Harry laughed, "For fifty-nine years of my life, I was pretty much under control. Then, for Christ's sake, during my sixtieth year I retired."

Harry told Tom the story of his retirement: the boredom, his being in the way of Alice Henrietta and her busy life, discovering—by accident—the office and the renewed energy it gave him, then Laura and everything that happened after their meeting. Two things he did not mention. Personal things. He did not speak of making love with Laura. He still didn't have that clear in his mind. And he didn't talk much about his private life with Alice Henrietta. Tom spoke of his conversation with her and how much he admired her work and her energy.

"I wanted to contact Alice as I was recovering," Harry said. "Let her know I was alive and where I was, but John discouraged me, and I went along with it. When I discovered who Laura really was I felt for Alice's safety—as well as mine. Thought any communication would be risky."

He stopped talking. Now he knew it would only be a matter of time.

Later they talked about Cami and Harry's chance meeting with her, laughing about the pest control business, and then about Tom's interview with her in South Dakota and then her death.

"I knew Cami wasn't being truthful with me," said Tom.

"I wonder how involved she was? If she was in it all the way. I mean involving me, if she really knew everything."

"That we may never know."

"Were they lovers?" Harry asked.

"With the feminist business, I wondered. Talking with Cami I thought so."

"I never got the feeling Laura hated men. Not in my relationship with her." He stopped, then added, "Got to stop calling her Laura. I <u>do</u> know she is tough, demanding. Not much warmth about her."

"She's totally focused on getting to the top," he continued. "To win, that's what I think. More than any mad lesbian, hate-men thing. And that could cause us a big problem."

"About the Coast Guard boarding John's boat, that bothers me. If John's right, it makes you think she either isn't convinced you're dead or is still seeking closure."

"Call Alice," Harry suggested. "Ask if anyone's made inquiries. If she told anyone about John's visit with her."

Tom called Alice the next morning. He discovered that an old friend of Harry's had called on Alice, a tall dark-haired lady in sunglasses fitting Victoria's description, and that Alice had mentioned to her the strange conversation with the Indian from Beaver Island. Tom's earlier suspicion was finally resolved. Still lingering within him had been the thought that Harry had tried to blackmail Leach with the discoveries he had made and that Victoria pushing him off the boat was actually Leach pushing him, trying to kill him.

Wasn't that the D.E.A.'s theory? Harry's repeated phone calls to the dealership had always bothered Tom. Now Harry's explanation that the calls had been made to coordinate Leach's trip to North Fox, the one on which Harry made the discoveries, cleared the suspicion. But it complicated the problem. There was only Victoria Nelson and Harry Jones. She would say that his mind was confused. The shock from extreme hypothermia. That would be easy for her. Hard for Harry to refute. How would they ever prove that Victoria Nelson tried to murder Harry Jones?

There was another problem lingering in Tom's mind, and he could not get a hold on it, and it would not go away. Tom needed to talk with Alice once more. A plan was being developed, and Alice, while not having full knowledge, had to be a part of it.

Tom did not want Alice to know just yet that Harry was alive. It was agreed upon. If she was questioned it would be almost impossible, they thought, for her not to seem disjointed, a little quirky. Common sense told Harry and Tom that it would take some time for Alice, who had just adjusted to a death, to discover that there wasn't a death after all.

Tom called Alice and told her to expect a call dealing with Harry's death and the drug business, an informal interview at best, and when it happened she must call him, that he had a plan. It was critical to the drug investigation. Alice agreed; she would call him, she would depend on him.

Then Tom asked. "Are you alright, Alice?"

"I'm fine. Why do you ask?"

"I just hope that what happened between us, well, you know... left you okay?"

"Sure it did," she replied. "I'm fine."

She ended it by saying, "You remember the old saying, Tom. We all try to be good, but not too good, and not quite all the time."

PART **FOUR**

It began with a light air of self discovery; it ended with the doomed reality of clinical depression. After her friend's death, she had met often with a respected psychiatrist at Walter Reed Hospital. Only this time it was different. He had called her. In his office he sat across a wide desk from his patient. He wanted contact: a hand on a shoulder or knee, even a clasp of hands. Her personality denied him that, instead he moved his chair around the desk and sat next to her. He offered a faint smile and was blunt.

"You are a manic depressive. You and I have discussed it; we've examined it, all of the symptoms are there, and that is where we are. I will prescribe medication. Probably you will use it the rest of your life... or some form of medication. You'll function normally. You have years upon years ahead of you—of very productive life."

She looked at him, almost as a stranger, and her first thoughts were that she didn't need an explanation of the pathology of depression. But she was not as indignant as she had planned. She knew the dynamics of depression, how the bottling up of one's problems, and the containment of stress led to feelings of hopelessness. But she needed the words, the proper description of those dynamics to make her less defensive. So she listened.

He paused. He had been looking down at his hands, as if he had been reading a script. Then he looked up at his patient and said, "I only wish you had closer friends, Victoria—your family, your brothers, but I'm not sure that's possible. But it would help if you had someone, not to pamper or appease, but someone to accept your situation and be strong with you about it."

He stood, putting his hands in his jacket pockets as doctors are want to do when the important, medical words run out.

"You have an associate, a peer, a fellow close to you in your work—Jim Bryant. Use him. He understands the problem. I treated his father for years. Before we knew how to handle the illness."

She stood up, turned her back to the doctor and moved several steps away. "I know Jim well, he's an excellent agent. And a friend," she added. "I just wish he'd stop trying to undress me everytime he looks at me."

The doctor, noticing her legs and figure, laughingly said, "He's probably not an exception to the rule. If you feel like talking, he's a listener. And he's a good family man, and he respects you." Pushing his chair back behind the desk he continued, "You're an exceptional person, Victoria. With a wonderful career ahead of you. It's your life, we all know that, but make it a great life, a rounded life."

He hesitated, "For the time being, we'll monitor this closely, watch your prescription. Help you with the nightmare. Then you'll be able to handle this yourself."

"Thank you," she said. She shook his hand firmly and left his inner office. Most of her questions had been answered.

Later that afternoon she returned to her office at the Drug Enforcement Agency in Arlington, Virginia. It was a large, grand office, a corner office with natural light, finely decorated with impersonal things. After years of noisy rooms full of running people, it had a quiet, sobering effect on her. It was a refuge for her. She didn't disagree with the doctor. She had read how a chemical imbalance often occurred, how it could impair her ability to function and—ultimately—the self-destruction it could cause. She glanced from the window to the picture on her desk. She and Cami standing in front of the nineteenth century brick home.

Her thoughts always returned to Cami Thurston. What she didn't realize was that although her love for Cami was real, as was Cami's for her, it also justified a greed within her—not only a sexual greed, but a professional greed as well.

Victoria took a yellow legal pad from her desk and stood in the light of the window. It was a speech she was reworking that she was to give three times later in the week in Miami, Los Angeles, and Chicago. Election time was near, and the administration, woefully short on a drug policy, needed priming. She didn't particularly like this facet of her job, but she was meant for it; a poised speaker, strikingly beautiful, with a credibility unequaled in the agency. There was a knock on the door and Jim Bryant poked his head into the room, a familiarity not shared by many. The glare of sunlight distinguished a female figure in the window.

"Victoria?"

"Yes."

"Alone?" It was almost burlesque.

Shadowing his eyes, peering behind the door. He asked "Everything okay?"

"Sure. You goofball, come in."

"No, really, I couldn't see you for the light. Do you have a second?"

"Sit yourself! I'm working on the speech."

She threw down the pad, dropped herself in her leather swivel chair, propped her legs on an open desk drawer and lit a cigarette.

"What's up?" she asked.

"Ever have an informant in Michigan named Harry Jones? Drowned himself."

"Name sounds familiar." She hesitated, "Harry Jones. It's one of those names though. We had a lot of help. I don't recall anyone drowning though. Why do you ask?"

"Weird thing. Guy could be alive."

"Drowned, but could be alive. Sounds reasonable to me." Inhaling the cigarette, she said, "Tell me more."

"Someone thought he was a D.E.A. agent. Got hold of our Grand Rapids, Michigan, office. They called me."

"Who? What someone?"

"An Indian was caught drunk, smoking pot, poaching deer on an island in upper Michigan. A game warden got him. The Indian didn't know a game warden from an F.B.I. agent and probably thought it might help if he had a story. Worked on a fishing boat for another Indian. Said he'd saved a drug agent named Harry Jones. Made a believer of the game warden, who told his boss; worked it's way up to me."

"Jesus!" she muttered to herself.

Jim caught it and turned to Victoria.

"Wasn't a Harry Jones the guy Jack Leach supposedly rubbed out. Some bit player in your drug deal?"

Victoria needed breathing room.

"I'll get on the computer. Go through my records, see what I can find out. Name Harry Jones sounds familiar. Probably the man you're talking about. Anything else?"

"No," Jim said, staring through Victoria. Preoccupied.

She looked up at him staring at her. "Suppose you have heard about my malady," she returned calmly, blowing smoke. "A manic depressive. That's what they call me."

"It's a doable. You'll handle it. Nothing really to hide.

We'll talk about it over coffee sometime."

Jim had a way of minimizing everything. He stood up, gave Victoria a short salute and left the room. He stuck his head back in, "Watch out for ghosts." Then slammed the door.

She sat at her desk, chin cupped in one hand, the cigarette touching an ashtray in the other. No one knew that Harry Jones was involved in the drug case except Cami and her. She was sure of that; not even his widow knew. He had assured her at the lodge in the Catskills that no one knew what he was doing. After his disappearance, there was not even a peep from the family. The detective Morgan had an idea, Cami had been sure of that, but in the end he felt Jones' involvement was with Jack Leach. She wished she had this information first hand, that Cami had taped their conversations, but it didn't happen, and that was that. She didn't know Morgan, but had no reason to think he had any knowledge of her relationship with Harry.

Could Harry be alive? He couldn't, he just could not have survived that water! But, Harry Jones? She shook her head, stood, walked to the window. She needed to send someone to Beaver Island. She needed someone to further interview Harry's widow. She questioned whether it had been smart to make that visit in the first place. She needed a confidant. Just one, and she knew of only one person and the one way to get him.

That night, after coffee, returning to her apartment and practicing her speech on Jim Bryant, she seduced him. He was nervous before and he was nervous afterwards.

He admitted it. Then he went home to his wife and three children.

Three days later, and coincidentally, the morning after she had taken him to bed for the third time, she called him into her office.

"Got a favor to ask of you."

"Sure."

"Remember the Harry Jones thing? You were right, supposedly he was drowned by the car dealer. Never proven. I think the prosecution dropped it to protect the main gist of the case. He could be important—really important—for putting Leach away."

"Leach that big?"

"Damned right he is!" Banging her fist on the table, she said, "It was a plea bargain… to get the business guys, the Mexican politicians, all those other big guys. But he was right in the middle of it."

"What's the favor?"

"I want you to track down the Indian story. Go to that island. But keep away from the local cops; I want it to stay in the agency. See what truth's in this Harry Jones thing. If he's alive, he could be big for us. Personally, I think it's a fantasy—some drunk Indian blowing smoke. But I want it quiet. Just the two of us, okay?"

"Right."

She wrote the word "retired" on her desk calendar. "Code name it 'retired.' That sounds good. I'll get you my itinerary. Leave a message each night on my answering machine. If you find something leave the word 'employed.' Follow up and keep in touch. If it looks like a dead end, just leave 'retired' and come home. Remember,' she asserted, "if anything develops, lets us get the credit. It's a little late for a new witness, but I want to cover everything."

"Not a witness like that," Jim laughed. "Coming back from the dead, walking into a courtroom. Jesus Christ, what a witness!"

"Thanks, Jim. I'd start with Harry Jones' widow... if I were you. I'll get you an address. Might just give you a feel for things."

She rose from the desk. He had been taking notes, then leaning forward said, "I didn't mention tonight. I don't think it would work out—Jenny and the children, you know."

For a second it was a blur to Victoria. Her thoughts were elsewhere. She recovered.

"That's no problem. I've got to shop tonight, anyway; spiff up for my speaking trip," she said with a slight smile. She started to walk Jim to the door and turned to him, "I didn't realize Jenny's family was such a huge supporter of the Democratic Party?"

"Her father and her father's father and his father. Hell, they probably built this place."

"Important folks," she said dryly. She nudged Jim in the ribs and said so long.

Jim left for Michigan with little more than the name of an Indian on Beaver Island and the address of the widow of a retired bookkeeper who apparently drowned through his involvement in a drug ring. To the common sense agent, the idea that he might be alive was intriguing but highly unlikely. Why Victoria was so interested was a question that blew by him, but he didn't delve on it—she had her reasons. She was a perfectionist for one thing. Never one to minimize a lead. He knew she had not risen to her level in the agency by making snap decisions, especially concerning tips, however goofy some might seem. Besides that, Victoria had asked him for a favor, really an order dressed as a favor, and that was important to him. He was aware, as were most at their level in the agency, that Victoria Nelson was for Victoria Nelson—first, last, forever. But his questioning apparatus had been temporarily consumed by his sudden, private, sexual interest in her.

Jim introduced himself to Alice Henrietta as Special Agent James R. Bryant, Drug Enforcement Administration. He had flown into Detroit metro several hours earlier. He was a tall, impressive looking man, but had a gentle face. A calming air about him. He was surprised how nervous she appeared and how careful she was in choosing her words. He knew nothing of what she might have known about her husband's activities; it was strange how some spouses knew everything about a partner's clandestine enterprises, others never a clue. He was suspicious, though. Partly it was the house, so stark, everything in place, it hardly appeared to be lived in—maybe tidied, arranged for his benefit, he thought.

"You *are* a housekeeper, Mrs. Jones. My wife surely could take a lesson."

"Oh, I'm a tidy one alright," Alice Henrietta returned. As if nervous, she stood and glanced through the kitchen window. "Never know when someone might come visiting."

"Let me ask you a question." He hesitated, wanting to put it right. "Are you satisfied that your husband, Harry, drowned last year?"

"I'm not *satisfied* that he drowned," she said dramatically. "I—."

"I'll rephrase that. May I call you Alice?"

"Yes." She re-seated herself, crossing her arms, fidgeting with her hands. Acting nervous.

"Alice, do you have any reason, any reason," he emphasized, "to think your husband could still be alive?"

"Alive! Alive," she restated. "Oh, my God. If I did, wouldn't you people be the first I'd want to speak to? Is there any reason I would not want to tell you, Mr. Bryant?"

She considered asking if she might call him Jim, but held back. She felt herself getting more defensive than she liked, perhaps flushed, so she stood again, and said, "Excuse me—if I go to the bathroom. I've had a regularity problem."

In the hallway she closed a portable phone in her hand, walked into the bathroom, and locked the door behind her.

When she returned the agent looked up from a notepad. He had been doodling with a ballpoint pen. She sat across from him and looked into his face, about chin level.

"I want to share something with you," she said.

"Please."

"Several months ago—maybe two and a half—my Master Charge showed two charges from Beaver Island, Michigan; I questioned the billing and I ask for receipts. They sent me photo copies in the mail." Alice Henrietta hesitated, looked away from the agent. She stood, more slowly now, and walked to the stove.

"I'm going to heat a cup of coffee. Like one?"

"Yes, thanks. And—?" The agent was gripped.

"The copies looked very much like Harry's signature."

"What did you do?"

"I paid them," she responded with a touch of innocence. "I'm investigating, of course."

"What were they for?" He was piqued.

"Cash. Drawn at a bank. For two hundred dollars each."

"They have a bank up there?"

"Evidently. I've never been there," she returned lightly.

"Do you have the copies?"

"No, I gave it all to a Mr. Thomas Morgan, a detective from Leland, who had been working on the case. He had interviewed me earlier about Harry's disappearance."

"You mean after Mr. Jones' boat was found?"

"I mean after the drug investigation was made public."

To Alice Henrietta, Agent Bryant looked confused. His next remark also contained a hint of frustration.

"Let me ask you—were you and Mr. Jones very close... in a loving sort of way?"

She bit her tongue. "In a loving sort of way?" she asked herself aloud. "No, I would say not. But after thirty-eight years, you know, there was a closeness."

He immediately wondered why he had asked the question. Was it her air of indifference?

"You don't have any records of the credit card transaction?" He asked with a doubting look.

"No, absolutely nothing. Let me call Mr. Morgan."

"No," he interrupted, "not at this time, Mrs. Jones. I would like you to do this." He stood and withdrew a card from his wallet. "This is me. I will be back with you, hopefully within several days. Please keep *my* visit and *our* conversation to yourself. I'm working on this. It's about your husband and his disappearance. Any outside interference at this time could jeopardize this. It could be extremely dangerous for all of us, for anyone concerned. With drug criminals it will take co-operation between all of us. Please say nothing until I contact you."

Jim Bryant was in a hurry. He shook hands, calling her Mrs. Alice Jones. Leaving his coffee steaming on the table, he dashed from the house. Among other things, he wondered why a detective would be investigating Harry Jones' disappearance after the drug case had been completed.

Alice Henrietta sat trembling. "I hope Mr. Bryant noticed this," she said, defiantly, watching her hands shake. She was not a nervous person, but the coffee tasted good. Tossing her head, she sighed aloud, "Oh, that Harry." Then she phoned her fellow crafters. There was work to be done. The fall shows were dangerously close at hand.

From the first pay phone Jim dialed Victoria's answering machine: Employed! Then he traveled north. The small car ferry rounded the lighthouse on Beaver Island. The agent suddenly felt he was somewhere else, perhaps in a New England coastal resort community. St. James Harbor was filled with anchored sailboats, from thirty-foot family cruisers to seventy-foot racers. Motor yachts crowded the marina, rafted three deep at the end of each finger pier. July and August were the months for boating in Michigan. Some were merely gunkholing among the bays and islands; others participated in the long sailing races that swept the lengths of Lake Huron and Lake Michigan. St. James seemed to amplify the spirit of the season; the small village of several hundred now swelled to several thousand. A communal spirit of freedom. The season for relaxing could be as strenuous and overindulged as work.

The agent shook his head, thinking of the earlier anxiety he had about melting into the small community. He felt lucky finding a seasonal bed and breakfast with a spare room. He pushed his way into the overcrowded, jostling, all-friendly Shamrock. A lady handed him her purse, she winked playfully as she flew off to dance. The bartender shrugged his shoulders, "That's what you get for having an honest face."

My kind of place, the agent thought, ordering up a Lite. My kind of assignment. Maybe he'd extend it a day or two.

It cost him a five spot, paid up front, for the tip and a nudge from a bar maid, "That's him. Kenny Little. The skinny one with the cap turned backwards, with the Bull's T-shirt."

Kenny Little and the other Indian, a bigger man with a ponytail, were drinking and laughing with subdued gestures, so Jim picked up his beer, handed the lady's purse to the bartender, and walked over to their table. He pulled out his billfold—if he needed to identify himself—and crouched down close between them. He looked at both and said, "My name's Jim Bryant, I'm from the Drug Enforcement Agency, the D.E.A. Can I speak with you?"

To his amazement the bigger man nudged him, stood up and said, "Let's go." He lead the way, followed by Jim and Kenny Little. The street was crowded with boaters and summer people and locals—all on a binge. Jim didn't feel intimidated as they knifed through the crowd, everyone milling, drinking, laughing. He wasn't easily intimidated anyway. It was less than a hundred feet to the water's edge. They stood looking at the boats, then at each other, all anticipating; the smaller Indian depended on his friend to speak.

The agent spoke first. "You are Kenny Little. You were poaching deer, drinking, smoking pot, got caught, and told a warden you'd helped save a guy named Harry Jones from drowning. Am I right?"

It was quick, to the point, and Kenny Little nodded.

Then the big Indian spoke, "I'm John Peltier." He held out his hand, and, innocently enough, he and the agent shook hands.

"We're drinking, he was poaching, and probably, facts known, we've all smoked pot one time or another. So let's cut the bull," Peltier said.

"Is Harry Jones alive?" Bryant shot back.

"As 'live as your old lady's muff."

"Where is he?"

"Tell you what, Mr. Agent, I've got to piss and Kenny here's got to piss. Right, Kenny?"

Kenny nodded right.

"Then we're gonna have a couple more beers. You join us for a couple beers. Then we'll talk business."

Just like that. Jim did a double take of the two, told them he needed to call his "old lady," telling her he'd arrived, and would meet them in the bar. He called the answering machine from the pay phone at the marina: Employed! Employed! Employed!

When he returned the Indians had lost their seats and were standing near a vintage 1950 jukebox at the far end of the bar near a rear door. John Peltier beckoned with a wave after the agent had spotted them. They had already ordered two Bud's and Jim ordered another Lite, watching as the bartender flipped off the cap. The bar was turning over with shouting and laughter. A four-piece band was set up on a make-shift stand behind the dance floor, and, when they started with "Irish eyes are smiling," people began singing, lowering the level of noise.

Jim watched the two Indians who in turn were watching everything. They seemed to be a part of this whole island event, gesturing to friends, occasionally peering above the dancers at the band.

"Always like this?" Jim shouted to John from a foot away.

"No," he yelled back. "July and August. That's it." He leaned closer so that he could be understood. "This is the big one—Fourth of July. Nothin' like it."

Jim thought it must be like Time's Square on New Year's Eve. All the excitement. John leaned forward again, "After Labor Day it's all over… finished. Lights out. Not five people in here. Just the locals. He looked at the agent, retrieving something, then turned, searching. He caught the eye of a barmaid, the one the agent had slipped the five.

"Emma," John shouted, as the hundred-and-fifty part harmony was winding down on an "Irish Lullaby." "Get us two," he said, holding up three fingers.

"And, Emma, he'll have one," John said, pointing to the agent, staring at her, winking at her. She caught it, nodded, and slipped through the crowd. She brought the beers, holding the necks between her fingers, two Buds for them, a Lite for the agent. The agent didn't notice the caps were off. The bar hushed, the band was playing *Danny Boy*. The crowd was singing; now they were all Irishmen.

The agent turned to John and asked, "About Harry Jones?"

"You want to see him?"

"Got to. That's why I'm here. See if he's alive or if Smokin Joe here's pulling someone's lariat." Jim was beginning to feel the excitement of the day.

"We'll see 'em in the morning when we ain't been drinkin'. He's scared, and I don't wanna scare 'em even more."

"Scared of what?" Jim raised his voice as the song ended, and the bar music turned up.

"Of gettin' killed!" John said. He turned to the agent, "For Christ's sake, someone trying to kill you and you ain't scared?"

"The drug people?" Jim asked, moving close to the Indian's ear. "They threatening him now? Threatening a possible witness? That's a federal crime. That's me!"

"Fuck no," John replied, close into his face. "Your lady friend. He didn't fall out of no boat; he was pushed."

The agent pulled back, unsure of what he had heard. Peltier beckoned him in close. "Your fuckin' lady drug agents tried to kill him."

"Bullshit!" Jim laughed, looking at his beer. He shook his head. The beer had gotten to the Indian, he was sure.

"Think he's lie'n," the Indian continued. "Why'd he fuckin' lie about shit like that. Fuckin' near died. We worked damn hard savin' his ass."

Jim looked up and knew the big Indian was neither drunk nor telling a tale. In a split second he knew the Indian could be wrong, but he knew he was talking from his heart. The next moment the agent thought the Indian's eyes began to haze, that the left side of his jaw started to pull up; his face was turning pale, and he believed the muscles on the Indian's neck were bulging.

"Yeah, tomorrow, we'll see him," the agent slurred as he

started to rise, and then he knew something was wrong and that the something was him. His legs were rubber bands—like once when he was a kid and had driven his jalopy without a muffler for four hours and stepped out and couldn't stand, and then he couldn't even wobble. He had fought it, and crawled into the house and fallen asleep on the kitchen floor. Afterwards, when he told the story, everyone said that was the worse thing he could do—stay out in the air and breathe the gas out, they said. So now he tried to fight it, but he couldn't. He felt their arms under his shoulders as they lifted him. He tried to use his feet, but they only slid across the dance floor to the rear door. Then they were out in the side alley, and to the agent everything became dark.

Jim Bryant was a big man, and he was fit. His head ached, as from a hangover, but he remembered where he had been, what had been said and exactly by whom. He also knew that he was now lying on his back, his hands atop his midsection, handcuffed, and his legs in leg irons. At first he thought he was on a waterbed, but the smell of fish and diesel fuel convinced him he was on a boat. He didn't think to worry what might have happened to him or about what could happen; he was just damned mad that he'd gotten himself into the predicament. The hand cuffs were roped to his legs, but the slack allowed him to pull the sheet from his face. Two men, neither of whom he knew, were sitting in white plastic lawn chairs. Both were past middle age, both with trimmed haircuts, both, frankly to him, looked like law enforcement people. He was half right. The bigger of the two smiled.

"Morning, mate."

The other, the smaller man, looking less confident, said, "You're not exactly who we expected."

"Then you know who I am?"

"We know what you are! You are an uncomfortable complication. That is what you are."

The shorter of the two stood up, exasperated.

"Let me ask you a question. How many people in this whole, wide, wonderful world know where you are this—this 'mornin after' morning in northern Michigan?" Harry raised his hand as if to interrupt himself. "Let me try to answer that question, myself. One. Maybe just one?"

"Maybe a hundred, maybe a thousand." Jim Bryant returned.

"Oh—? She would have a thousand confidants in the D.E.A.," Harry said sarcastically. "Told a thousand agents she pushed Harry Jones out of the back of a boat in the middle of freezing Lake Michigan, and left him there to drown." He whistled aloud shaking his head. "Then a question arose about him surviving and a legion of you were sent to check it out. Right?"

"You guys have this all wrong—whoever you are," the agent returned. He squirmed on his side so that he was now sitting up. Confidently, he continued. "You and those Indians are all fucked on this thing."

At that moment John Peltier arrived, stuck his head in the cabin, "Ready boys, we're off for High Island." The diesel turned slowly, as though out of sync, then they were moving.

"You guys are all screwed up on this," Jim said.

"How many know you're here? How many? I'm asking you. How many will come before she comes looking for you?" Harry asked.

The agent shrugged. "Maybe she—they," he caught himself.

"Maybe *they* don't know anything about this," the taller man interjected.

Fear struck Jim Bryant for the first time. Could these be drug people setting up Victoria or setting up the agency for a revenge killing for Jack Leach, or the Mexicans, or the New York people. It had been known to happen. Their wealth had taken the logic out of everything they did. A quick panic.

"Who are you guys? Where are we going? Is Harry Jones *really* alive? Your friend, the Indian, said I'd see him today."

"You're looking at him, pal," said the shorter man.

A drained, confused feeling shot through the agent. He sat looking at the two of them. The fear that was first in his mind and then in his stomach left him. Reprieve granted; death gone; life returned. He turned aside, tried to be sick to his stomach, but he felt empty, and dry-heaved. And he didn't feel any embarrassment about it at all.

Tom turned to his friend. "Sea sick, or a tough night… or both. Tell John to have his helper clean this up. I'll get your friend an apple." Harry looked at the agent and pointed to Tom. "This is Tom Morgan. A detective from Leland helping me out. Incidentally, your gun is in safe hands."

That was the first time Jim thought about his compact pistol. They sat him in a chair wedged into a corner, water in one hand, apple in the other. The boat rolled from the cross waves. There wasn't anything, he thought, he'd done right on this trip yet. Except maybe his phone contacts with Victoria's answering machine. The two men sitting with him were quietly eating apples. Their thoughts seemed beyond Jim Bryant. Was this really Harry Jones, he asked himself. Could he have recovered from a near-death situation and be confused by the circumstances that surrounded the experience. "Why would Victoria Nelson want to kill you?" he asked.

"That's what the hell I'm trying to find out," said Harry, looking at the agent. "Were you ever part of the case?"

"I knew a lot about it."

"She ever talk about me? About how I discovered the landing field on North Fox? How I found out where the drugs came from? How they got to Jack Leach Chrysler?"

"She knew about the island and the air strip."

"How'd she know?"

"Old reports. A drug raid over there years ago."

Tom Morgan knew that, but let it pass.

"Did Victoria tell you how she discovered the drugs in the cars from Mexico?" Harry continued.

"No, she didn't. I suppose it was an anonymous tip."

"Fuckin' anonymous tip, my ass." Harry stood up, catching a grab rail. "I'm the son-of-a-bitch who should be puking his guts. She never mentioned the name Harry Jones?"

"Never to me."

"And you knew her well?"

"I knew her well. I *know* her well," he defended.

"Not a little self-serving, is she? Not just a little I-me-ish?" he returned, again sarcastically. "Not me! Me! Me! At all costs. Not Victoria and Cami! Me! Me! Me! And the hell with everyone and everything else?"

He paused, staring at the agent.

"Not so much Cami," the agent muttered, but in defense of Victoria he added, "what the hell, we're all I—me guys to some degree."

"Thank you very much for that," Harry said, cutting him off.

There were several moments of silence. Harry and Tom said nothing, neither did Jim. They were looking at Jim, but Jim was looking away, searching, in his own thoughts.

Finally, Harry said, "I want to ask you one question." Harry looked at Jim, and Jim returned the stare. "Just one question," Harry said. "For one little answer." He paused, "Was it on the Q.T? Victoria asking you to check this out for her? For the agency, no one else involved? No police agencies, no inquires, just hush, hush. Just you and her. Maybe a third. Somebody really close to her. And if I were alive, and this wasn't any bullshit drunken Indian half-assed story, what was she going to do then? What was going to happen? Was she going to fuck you like she did me, ask you to forget it, and let her handle it her way?" He paused.

Harry sat down in the chair glaring at Jim Bryant. Tom Morgan looked at Harry, stood, waited for an answer that didn't come and stepped into the cabin. He returned a few seconds later with three apples and gave one to the sullen agent.

"That's what she did with me, you know. When I met her in the Catskill Mountains, told her the whole story, everything I'd found out about the drug case—from Jack Leach to North Fox Island, from the Chrysler dealership to Toluca, Mexico."

Later, the two of them stood on the deck as the trawler neared High Island. Tom turned to Harry.

"When you were talking about Victoria and you in the Catskills?"

"Yes?"

"And what she'd done?"

"Yes?"

"You were talking figuratively?"

"No."

"Literally?"

"Yes."

"You never told me that."

"I don't recall you asking."

A moment of silence followed, then Harry turned to his friend. "Some things are just as well left unspoken." He grinned, nudging his friend, as the movement of the boat pulled them apart.

"Don't you agree?" Harry asked.

"Guess you have a point," Tom answered, dryly, and that ended it.

They anchored in an open bay on the northeast side of the island. The bay was the shape of a half moon, a thousand yards wide, rimmed by a white sand beach. The beach was hard sand for seventy feet, then rolling dunes of soft sand, then the forest. The island was covered with hardwoods and conifers and birch. No one lived on the island. There was no electricity, only an abandoned Conservation Corp's cottage, deep in the woods, fronted by a small lake that was more of an overgrown pond of water lilies than a lake.

They transported their chained captive to the beach in a large working dingy full of wet nets and roping. The five of them trudged slowly over a small sand dune along a trail that became a pine-covered path as it lead into the woods.

"See that," John Peltier said, looking at Jim and pointing to the vines that climbed high into trees. "It's poison. If you're sensitive, it'll damn near kill you. Took a party over here fishing, three ended up in the hospital. Never seen sumac grow so high."

They came to the cottage, banged through the screened porch, and walked in. It was dark from the heavy foliage surrounding it. There were two cots. Blankets were neatly piled in the middle of the floor. Two wooden fruit crates with bags of food sat on a sink counter.

"This is home," Tom said. "There isn't going to be any bullshit, friend. This is going to last as long as it has to last. There's no electricity on the island. There's no one living here. Kenny has no keys to unlock you. No phone to call for help. He's got a stun gun, and he knows when to use it. Don't intimidate him. No use you or anybody getting hurt. You're not the big kahona of this deal, so it's nuts getting hurt.

Tom turned from the agent to Kenny. "The mosquitoes are hell out here. At least the black flies are over. Screens look pretty good, though." He started to leave, and for the agent he added, "John will be checking. He fishes off this island."

The agent, sitting in the chair, repeated what he said earlier, "I still think you got this thing all wrong."

"You think about it," Tom said. "You've got time to think about your friend Victoria Nelson. You put it together!"

They left. The agent was seated in a corner with a plastic bottle of distilled water. Across the room, at a distance, sitting erect, was Kenny Little and his stun gun. Neither showed much interest for the other. Nothing was said of the handheld V.H.F. they had hidden for Kenny, nor was any mention made of how they had painstakingly instructed him on activating a battery-rigged tape recorder that Tom and Harry had installed the previous day.

Walking back to the boat, Harry turned to Tom, "You think he's more on ethics and the drug agency than he is on Victoria Nelson, don't you?"

"I hope so," Tom said. "It would make this whole thing a lot easier."

"Hope we don't end up with an island full of agents."

Tom snorted, laughing in a serious sort of way.

"I don't think so. 'Course I didn't expect this 'Jim,' either."

After a pause, Harry returned, "she won't be telling many people about this thing. I know her that well."

Victoria Nelson expected a new response on her answering machine, was that not the plan? She knew no one to call. She had learned long ago never to call a spouse, it multiplied problems. She ate dinner in her hotel room, watched TV, reviewed the speech as she had delivered it, looking for improvement, and then tried her answering machine again. She would call in the morning before her flight to Los Angeles.

The following evening, about the time Harry and Tom were to have dinner at the Beaver Island Lodge, Victoria flew to Chicago. She stayed in a hotel at O'Hare International. She had booked a flight directly to Dulles the following afternoon. That had been her plan. For the second night there was nothing from Jim Bryant on her answering machine. She called a D.E.A. switchboard; Agent Bryant was on assignment for an undetermined period, Ms. Nelson. He had been on assignment for several days, Ms. Nelson.

Meanwhile, Glenallen, having been asked to have dinner with Tom at the lodge, sat down at the table with Tom and a stranger, was introduced by Tom who pointed to the stranger, saying without fanfare, "This is Harry Jones, I think you've met." As Glenallen said later, he looked at the bearded man, took a double-take, peered into his eyes, and was Godstruck.

"Goddamned Godstruck, I was."

After hearing the story, it was impossible for him to believe Harry had been resurrected right under his nose. Tom knew Glenallen had to be in the fold, Victoria and Cami had interviewed him during the drug investigation and the detective was sure she would seek him out now that she'd be searching for the agent.

She canceled her flight from Chicago. After her speech she had returned to her room, dialed a blank on her machine and knew something was wrong. Renting a car she drove north along the Michigan coastal Highway 31, reaching Charlevoix after midnight. She got a room for the night, and, in a third call, she located the bed and breakfast where Jim was staying. His bag and personal items were there, but the proprietor had not seen him for two days. Victoria flew to Beaver Island in the morning on a small commuter plane. At the bed and breakfast, she informed her hostess that she'd be using Jim Bryant's room until he returned, then she would be leaving. She had a way that left little margin for rebuttal. Besides, this was Beaver Island and Jim's room wasn't even locked. Nothing in the room suggested anything, except a note on the night table with the names Alice Jones and Kenny Little crossed off, and the name Jenny with "gift" after it not crossed out. Victoria turned cold for a moment, then shut it off.

Glenallen's back was to her as she stepped into the office at the Municipal Marina. He was talking to a boater somewhere out in Lake Michigan on his V.H.F. radio. He turned and recognized her with a slight waver.

"I'll hold the slip. Go around the north end of the pier— north end. I'll be standing there to assist. Beaver Island Municipal Marina, out."

"Hi stranger," he greeted Victoria. "Knew you'd fall for Beaver Island. Got in your blood, didn't it?"

"You might say that."

"Loners. They like it the best."

"What makes you think I'm a loner?"

"I just thought—."

"Thanks. Fact is I'm looking for a friend. Tall guy, reddish blond, light complexioned. Looks like he'd burn easy. Seen him?"

"Awful lot of people up here now."

"I planned to get here earlier," she said. "He's been around a couple days."

Glenallen looked at Victoria, she looked agitated. He spoke deliberately. "Saw a fellow might fit that description. Talking to Kenny Little, the Indian."

He hesitated. "They might have gone fishing. Kenny guides a lot. 'Course I haven't seen either of 'em for a couple days."

"Would they stay overnight?"

"Some do. Some of the islands have cabins on 'em. Make for good fishin' camps. None of the islands 'cept Beaver has people on them. Lots of fish, but no people."

He excused himself. She watched him walk bowlegged out to the dock. More of a waddle. A large motor yacht rounded the lighthouse steering for the marina. After he returned, he said, "Fact is, you might see John Peltier. He supplies the camps."

"John Peltier?" The name rang a note.

"Tall Indian. Can't miss him. Wears a ponytail. See the trawler over there, the Janet E.," he said, pointing to the other side of the harbor. "That's him. Commercial fisherman. He fishes for a living. He's a good man. A good, honest man."

Glenallen knew about the Coast Guard boarding John's boat looking for drugs. He suspected she knew and he gave her a shot, but she didn't flinch.

"Where does he live?" she asked. "I'll give him a try. Just like Jim to go off fishing."

"Up behind the post office. Two blocks and you'll see a group of shacks. The first one. Has a glass porch on the backside. I'd check the Shamrock first, though. Sittin' in the back if he's there."

She smiled. "Nice to see you again, Glenallen."

"Yeah. Knew you'd be back, though. Island has a way with people."

He waved, and she cursed herself for thinking about a double meaning. She didn't think Glenallen was playing with her mind. Nor did she feel any undercurrent of evil about the island. She was sure places like this make outsiders feel like outsiders. She had been told there were four thousand on the island now, in the winter less than four hundred. If Harry Jones had been saved, where was he? If this Kenny had saved him, people must know. And what about the other Indian? It wouldn't be long before everyone knew she was here, she thought. She should have inquired about Harry Jones, just in passing. She would speak to Glenallen again, later, but now Victoria was most interested in locating Jim Bryant.

John Peltier was in the bar, sitting with a large woman in an apron. A cook. The Shamrock was full in the middle of the day. It was the only place in town to drink that was near the boat docks. She sat down next to Peltier. She had sensed him watching her from the moment she entered. She wore a long-sleeved khaki shirt, khaki pants, and hiking boots. The shirt had tabs on the sleeves and two buttons through flap pockets above her breasts. It had split raglan sleeves. Fishermen called it a casting shirt. He acted surprised when she seated herself. The cook moved from the table.

John smiled at her. "You're looking for a fishing guide, I bet?"

"Actually," she said, "I'm looking for a fisherman."

"I'm a fisherman. How can I help?"

"I mean a particular fisherman."

"Lost one?"

"You might say that. You know Kenny Little?"

"Kenny works for me. I mean, when Kenny wants to work, he works for me."

"You mean to say he's not too reliable."

"I mean to say he's got other things going. Been staying out on High Island. He's a loner. Gets in a mood for being alone sometimes."

"Seen him with a big tall guy? In his thirties?"

"No, Kenny's probably alone. Kind of that way—." John continued slowly along a trail that seemed to be wandering nowhere. "Still," he continued, "I drop off rations for him… took more food than one guy needs. What with Kenny fishin' and poachin' and everything."

"You go all the way out there for him?"

"No. I fish that water. Have nets out there."

"Can you contact him? Does he carry a V.H.F.?"

"No."

"You'd think he would, for safety's sake."

"You'd think so."

He turned and poured himself another cup of coffee from the glass pot brewing behind him on a shelf.

"Have a cup, Miss?"

She nodded, and he stood up, getting her a clean cup. Victoria studied him. He was big, but clean-shaven. Someone had recently trimmed his hair. He smelled of burned wood and wore a plaid shirt; warm for the season, but clean, and, she thought, probably what he wore all year long. He sat back down, this time across from her. He rested his chin on one hand. He wasn't looking at Victoria and was talking as if thinking aloud.

"More I think, the only tall guy I've seen Kenny with was Tom. No thirty-year-old, though. Tall, gray-haired, like sixty-plus. An old detective from Leland. Comes up fishing sometimes. Yeah, Kenny was talking with Tom. I didn't see him with any big guy in his thirties." He looked at Victoria. She had been staring into the crowd, but listening to what he said. She felt a sudden need to confront him about Harry Jones, but she didn't want to alarm him. She needed to find Jim Bryant. Was Tom Morgan involved? Could Jim have somehow tied in with Tom Morgan looking for Harry Jones? Or had Morgan also heard the rumor started by the Indian and decided to investigate? Had Jim and the retired detective accidentally crossed paths? For the first time Victoria wondered if she should have sent him up here. She needed to talk to Kenny.

"When are you taking supplies to Kenny?" she asked.

"Tomorrow."

"I want to go. Maybe they're out there together. My friend's a real fisherman."

"Set your clock. I leave out about four-thirty."

"I'll be there," she tapped his arm. "Thanks for the coffee," and left the Shamrock.

"No problem," he said to himself, aloud.

He rose, turning to the cook. "Need to use the phone, Emma," he said.

Moving to the kitchen, his biggest concern was that the lady who had come looking for Jim Bryant might ask around and discover that it was he and Kenny who had "helped" the guy out of the bar. The town was so busy though, that's as far as it could go, he thought. He called Tom and Harry at the Lodge. After tomorrow morning, it wouldn't matter.

What was happening to her? She thought about Harry Jones and Jim Bryant. She didn't think this had somehow turned bad, though she knew full well that no one was beyond killing. Harry? Not Harry. She couldn't see him

involving himself in violence. Something could have happened with Harry, she thought, to make him psychotic, to
make him snap. Fear itself, considering the first attempt on
his life, if it had failed, could be a logical motive. It might jus-
tify a violent act. She was getting ahead of herself. She wanted to shrug it off because she could find no explanation for
him surviving in that water.

She hoped Tom Morgan was involved; the more
involved, the less likely a violent confrontation. For her sake
she didn't need that to happen.

And what if Harry Jones was alive? The bottom line was
that she felt she had handled the whole business with Harry
so well that no one would believe whatever story he were to
tell. She considered the irony in it. Part of the reason she was
covered was because Harry accomplished so much without
her. She had conceded that to him.

She made a call to her answering service. Again, there
was nothing from Jim Bryant.

There was a dead calm in the harbor when Victoria
stepped onto the dark street at 4:25 a.m. A light fog had
formed above the water, muffling the early morning plead-
ings of the gulls. She had covered her shoulders with a
Gore-Tex rain jacket and fitted her hair into a billed cap. She
carried a compact Beretta in one of the two zipped pockets,
an Icon V.H.F. in the other. As she walked, her back was to
the marina, and she didn't notice the Coast Guard rescue
boat moored at the municipal dock.

A short, disheveled Indian that Victoria did not recognize was helping John Peltier load empty crates on the back

of the trawler. She stepped aboard, he looked up, nodded, and, when she asked if she could help, he pointed forward and said there was fresh coffee in the cabin. Filling two Styrofoam cups she returned to the open deck. He watched her as she approached. John took one cup and spoke.

"Fog can spook you if you're not used to it."

"I've been in it before," she said. "Will it clear?"

"Sun should burn it off. Maybe patches later. Fog's not bad so long as you got radar. Can see through anything with good radar."

There was a moment of silence.

"Small boats?" She asked.

"If you're lucky."

There was a pause as he continued working.

"We'll head south between North and South Fox, pull those nets, then head up for High and the nets on the south end. Kenny stays on the northeast corner in a bay. We'll anchor off, take Kenny's supplies ashore in the dingy. I usually just leave 'em," he added. "But I'll point the direction; you can go check on your friend, see if he's there."

To Victoria the engine seemed reluctant at first, but then it smoothed out. The gulls picked up the movement as the boat crept out of the harbor by the lighthouse. They weren't screaming as they do on the return. Just quietly following. She shuddered from the cold, damp air. A suspicion had grown in her about the fisherman. She was sure he knew more about her than she knew about him. He threw her a life jacket as he steered.

"Wear this. Never know when you might end up in the water."

He paused, then looked back at her. She was standing in the cabin watching the radar screen.

"You're good for about forty-five minutes out there," he said, pointing to the water. "Maybe an hour and a half —tops."

"Couldn't you swim?" she inquired. "Make it to shore?"

"In this close, maybe. Not five or six miles out. Too cold. Get exhausted. You know about hypothermia?"

"Yes," she said. "I know."

Steering into the fog, John kept a close eye on the radar. She pulled his free arm down, checking the empty cup. She filled it, inquiring about his companion.

"He brings his own. I do enough for him. I pay him. He's not all there. I'm the only one who gives him work."

"A native?" Victoria asked.

"Not a native. Came from a reservation on the mainland. Lives with a family here." He paused, then added, "We help our own. No one else interested."

"Is Kenny a native?"

"No. But he's been on the island for ten years."

"Does this 'Tom' fish with Kenny?" She asked.

"Hell, no. He fishes with a friend. A cop from Charlevoix."

If Kenny didn't know where Jim was, she thought, Tom Morgan did know. She would travel to Leland next. Maybe Jim had already gone there. But why hadn't he contacted her? She recognized North Fox as they motored past. The fog was now gone, and the morning sun glared across the water and made the long sand beach even whiter against the dense forest. She had flown over North Fox during the investigation, long before Harry Jones had made his discoveries there.

Later, they anchored off High Island in the northeast corner of the bay. Victoria was surprised when John said he'd motor her ashore, drop the box of supplies on the beach and let her check out the cottage, pointing to the general direction in the forest, and that he would wait for her on the trawler.

"There's a path. Don't know why Kenny didn't answer the horn." He had blasted his horn as he said he usually did, and Kenny had not appeared.

"I don't like to leave this guy alone on the boat. He gets fidgety, has a time warp, begins to think he's a little kid and starts playing with stuff."

Her first thought was that she was being set up.

"Where do you think he is?" She asked.

"I'd guess fishin'. There's a small lake just in from the trees beyond the C.C. cottage. You'll see it."

She turned to him. "I've a handheld." She pulled it from her jacket pocket. "Monitor me on channel 16. That way the Coast Guard can be listening in, too. Just so we're all on the level here." She knew he was already using Channel 16, the Coast Guard monitoring station. They jumped into the dingy and motored the hundred and fifty feet to shore. He carried the box up the beach and returned to the dingy.

"Be waiting," he said.

"See you, pal," she replied. She had not mentioned to him about her Beretta. On the beach, she felt completely vulnerable and quickly walked through the sand into the dunes. The path was exactly where John had said. She was relieved when it became woods. Once there, all noise ceased to exist. The surf was gone, as were the cries of the sea birds. A crow called, and she pulled back the receiver on the small pistol, loading a shell into the chamber. The cottage was within fifty yards. She waited next to a screened window that was open. No sound, she peered in and saw Jim Bryant in a chair, bound, nodding into sleep. She hesitated, pistol in hand, then neither hearing nor seeing anyone else, slipped through the front door. Jim's head jerked up.

"Where is Kenny?" She whispered.

"He left last night." Jim said loudly. "You can talk. No one here but us."

It was as if he had expected her to walk into the cabin at any moment.

"How'd he leave?"

"Probably Peltier picked him up."

"Little guy?"

"No, tall, skinny."

"Should have figured something," she said. "We may be missing a ride off this place."

"How did you get here?" Jim asked.

"Peltier and his fishing boat."

"A setup," he murmured, shaking his head. Victoria was standing in front of Jim. He looked up defiantly.

"You told me somebody drowned Harry Jones. Or tried to drown Harry Jones. Jack Leach—the drug guy—I think you said. Isn't that what you said?"

He pulled in his chained legs and stood awkwardly. He shuffled toward the door. "I've got to piss," he said in a low voice, then turned back to her, angrily.

"You forgot to tell me you were the one who pushed him off a boat in fifty degree water… to die in Lake Michigan."

"Then he is alive." She stated it as fact.

There was silence.

He started to speak, but she interrupted him. "You don't know anything about this, Jim. Why do you need to know why all this happened? Who will people believe? Things happen to memories after periods of unconsciousness. The doctor and I talked about it. People recover differently. Hypothermia… who knows?"

Jim cut Victoria off. "All I know is that he's alive. Regardless of what happened or didn't happen, whether it was planned, who planned it, or what was supposed to happen. It happened, and he is alive. It happened!" He shouted, "Period!"

He continued, "We live within a perimeter, Victoria. Do you understand that?" He was fatigued, but he was being very deliberate. "We work within a very defined perimeter. And we live within one—one and the same. They have to relate to the other. Inside one big circle. Your conscience is the same conscience; your personal life, your professional life—all the same damned thing."

There was a momentary lapse of words, then Victoria returned, "They will believe me." At first she was emphatic, then with something less, she looked at him and calmly said, "I think you'll grow to understand why I thought as I did, given the circumstances, and why things happened... about Cami and me and about our particular relationships with the agency."

"Listen to me, Victoria," he interrupted. "Someday I'm going to retire. I want to retire with honor, with a family who not only loves me, but respects me. Who looks up—." He stopped. "Maybe not a hero thing, but damned well with respect."

She had not been listening. Looking him squarely in the eyes, she said, "You'll understand because you are an understanding person. You have compassion. You've come with that from your kind of upbringing, I guess."

"And...," she added, "You have a great wife and family. The whole thing."

For only a second the thought of their short, sudden relationship shot into his mind and its consequences, then he stumbled out of the cottage and relieved himself. He was dazed by what he had just gone through with Victoria.

She followed him into the woods. "Let's see if we got a ride. How'd you get here?"

"Same way you did. But they knocked me out with a drink. Stupid! Woke up in the fishing boat staring at Harry Jones and Tom Morgan. Heard the whole thing. No one was combative. Just practical, pissed-off people trying to figure what the hell's going on. They figured you'd come alone... not wanting to tell anybody what happened."

"Wonder if I'd sent someone else?"

"Then I'd had company." He stopped, but couldn't refrain from adding, "Guess they figured you couldn't fuck everybody."

She said nothing.

They left the forest; Victoria was now leading the way through the dunes toward the beach when she stopped dead in her tracks.

In the bay, close by the shore, sat a Coast Guard rescue craft moored near the fishing trawler. Facing her were two uniformed men. To Victoria's left were the three fishermen, staring at her, as were the two men, a hundred feet away, on her right. The tall man she did not recognize, but the shorter man, by his build, even with the beard, she knew was Harry Jones.

A Coast Guardsman, the officer, yelled from the beach, "Come to offer you a ride back." She waved a salute. The only thing that seemed appropriate.

Tom Morgan watched Victoria and thought about Cami Thurston. He had actually liked Cami. She had fooled him, he knew, but he also knew you could still like people who fooled you—it happens a million times in a million relationships every day. But there was something about this Victoria that he knew was not like Cami. He doubted that her father was a farmer, or that she knew she had a smoking problem, or that she thought she ever had any problem at all. She glanced casually at Tom, then moved toward Harry, angling him so that he moved away from Harry and her.

She stopped three feet in front of Harry. She started to offer a hand, but thought that was moot and didn't know what to do or what to say. She merely dropped her arms and looked into his face.

"You know," Harry said quietly, "right now, right here, at this moment, I don't feel very good about myself."

"You should, Harry Jones. I'll give you that. You should."

Once again there was a sense of sarcasm. This time it did not go unrewarded.

"I never really liked you," he said. "I never really

wanted to like you. But you were a challenge." He paused, raising his chin slightly. "Isn't that what we all want? It's damned well what we need. It is what people my age need—to get us above the ordinary things. The ordinary is too easy for people like me to accept. I've accepted that all my life."

Harry stopped talking, and there was nothing more to say.

POST**SCRIPT**

She did not remember ever being in such a high state of anxiety. Perhaps on her wedding night. Then he entered the house. He was still bearded, but now trimmed, and with one hand she held the back of his neck as he kissed her. And the tenseness did not leave her. She had prepared a candle light dinner. They were both nervously happy and there were hours of conversation that for a time held them apart. Alice Henrietta also had her triumph, and Harry Jones had never felt such genuine interest for her work. He kept coming back to it. Scattered throughout the house were dozens of weathered window frames, all wooden, so roughly unkempt they appeared to be old barn windows; mostly four pane, a few six pane. In many the glass was cracked, in others missing completely. The wooden grids, all intact, were bleached from age. Yet, they were complete. Behind each frame was an image; vague country settings of barns and meadows, seascapes with lighthouses, ponds with water lilies, all painted in oil on Masonite backing. There was an adventure about each of them; one wanted to rub clean the glass so that an imagination could be fulfilled. They were the highlight of every show. So many special orders for so many individual imaginations that new ladies were added to Alice Henrietta's illustrious group. Her triumph.

Harry would see little of Tom Morgan. Tom Morgan hadn't tried to initiate a closer relationship, and Harry was not a fisherman, and he did not like to reminisce with others and really was still a loner. Harry felt Tom knew that about him and left it at that, but one night he did get a call. Tom Morgan had been informed that shortly before an inquest was to convene, the body of Victoria Nelson was found in the cemetery in Vermillion, South Dakota. A suicide. An associate, a male agent in the D.E.A., stated publicly that she had been despondent, never recovering from the death of a friend. No one seemed surprised, least of all, Harry Jones.

Harry kept his office and spent a good deal of time there. He found a purpose for his word processor: he would put down, as best he could, the short history of his retirement. He would write a story! It would be written as fiction, but it would be based in fact. The names of the characters would be fictitious except for the two harbormasters. The country would be real.

Sept. 3, 2003
Beaver Island